NEXT OF
KIN

ELTON SKELTER

ISBN: 9781590217764

Front cover design by Elton Skelter
Interior layout by Inkspiral Design

Published by Lethe Press

"*Next of Kin* is a heartbreaking romance for the depraved. Skelter's use of perspective paints a complex portrait of the two utterly broken characters at the center of this twisted tale. Its themes of longing, abuse, and loss of control make this a timeless piece of queer horror."
CAT VOLEUR, author of *Revenge Arc*

"Gay as hell. Love, murder, sex, gore, humor, *Next of Kin* has it all."
N.J. GALLEGOS, author of *The Broken Heart*

"Elton Skelter's *American Psycho* on Zoloft: that boundary-crossing transgressiveness is there, but Skelter's novel is more buoyant with a beating bloody heart."
NICK CUTTER, author of *The Troop*

"Fans of Poppy Z. Brite's *Exquisite Corpse* will especially want to check this out."
PUBLISHERS WEEKLY

"Skelter's work moves quickly, alive with sex, violence, and plot twists."
KIRKUS REVIEWS

PART ONE:

We Are Each
Our Own Devil

(OSCAR WILDE)

JACOB MALLORY:

HELL FOR THE COMPANY

MARK TWAIN

CHAPTER ONE

I'M ON A DATE IN this 4000 square foot TriBeCa loft, and he
has a waiter bring the starter to the table, who I am guessing
doubles as the chef by the slight finger-shaped stains down
the sides of his white kitchen coveralls. The table is too long
for two and likely made from some refurbished flotsam from
some maritime shipwreck, the Mary Celeste or the Titanic.
If I asked, he would probably explain condescendingly how
it is and is not made with wood from the ship of Theseus.
Either way, it no doubt cost more than my entire mortgage.

His voice carries across the room, and he says: "de
Blasio dyes his hair. I lost all respect for the man when the *Post*
dropped he uses that crap in a box." He shovels the appetizer,
a raw oyster drowned in a meek algae-colored sauce, into
his mouth with the wrong fork. And he says, "Gray hair is
supposed to be distinguished. Not that I voted for the guy.
When I'll need it, I'll see Pompey in Midtown West."

I sigh and move the langoustine around the plate with
the right fork, smear the sauce to the left with the fish slice,

and feign eating by spreading it out wide across the far-too-large dish.

And he's asking: "Do you play sports?"

He says: "I play a bit of golf in my downtime, spend a good deal of time on the back nine of the country club. My father's a member, and he can get us in. Just say when."

I ask: "If you had to choose, how would you like to die?"

I'm not a quiet man, but the words fall on deaf ears as he wipes the muck-green mulch from his goatee with the Egyptian cotton napkin that's more indulgent than my sheets back home.

The waiter clears the plates, tops off the wine, and disappears in a puff of disinterest.

My date then grins at me from the head of the table, flecks of brown stuck in the crowns of his enamel veneers, and he says: "I'm glad you could come. It's nice to have company when it's been a bitch of a day."

And I ask: "Suffocation or exsanguination?"

He just nods and straightens the remaining knives and forks, none of which he understands the purpose of, and asks: "Almost forgot what you do. I'd hate to be in corporate real estate these days."

I do not work in real estate. It's graphic design, but I don't correct him.

The waiter brings the next course and, with a wrapped hand, places the steaming dish in front of first him and then a second plate in front of me. It's chicken whatever, piled too high on a miniature mound of mashed ube. All I can smell is aniseed, which turns my stomach. Nonetheless, the scent is a break from the smell of tonka bean and cedar wood, leather and library books.

The waiter does not meet my eyes. I am grateful as he leaves, but I don't thank him. An evening out on a first date, should all be thankless.

I take another sip of the wine: red, mid-quality, but slightly corked. I can't tell if it tastes good, my knowledge doesn't extend that far, but it's enough that it doesn't taste vinegary.

My date is carving chicken with a steak knife and chewing with his mouth open. Then, through the morsels of masticated meat, he asks: "Did you hear about Brian and Terrence?"

I say: "I don't know who the fuck Brian and Terrence are," and drink another gulp of wine.

"Well, funniest thing: Brian made a bad investment in some kind of scheme. Turned out to be Ponzi or pyramid. One of the two. Terrence has him sleeping in the garage." He laughs.

I don't eat the food. I drink more and notice from my periphery, as I eyeball the embarrassment at the opposite end of the table, that the waiter returns and tops off my glass right to the rim. I lay a hand on his forearm, and he leaves the bottle with a nod, never quite meeting my eye.

There's a movie poster on the wall behind my date featuring the engorged head of a mature Affleck, one of the nameless brothers, and it looks like it's been signed.

"Would your father miss you if you died?" I ask, and he takes another mouthful of chicken thigh, slaps his lips together, grinds the meat down.

He says: "You're quite handsome, actually. But not my usual type."

I look at him vacantly and nod. He doesn't notice the motion.

He tells me he met Abigail Breslin in Le Bernardin, ran into Sandra Bernhardt on Broadway, shared a cab with Benicio Del Toro to a party in the Meat Packing District. None of this sounds remotely true, but the look he has in his eyes when he announces this to the room, I'm sure he believes his own hype.

If I left, he might sit there and continue to eat like a hog, regaling an imaginary captive audience of one, loudly and ostentatiously through the cavernous loft, and not notice I was gone until I was back on street level in the winter chill, hailing a cab out front.

The waiter clears the dishes, his plate is a war zone, and mine is untouched, the cold chicken thighs sliding down a moistened mountain of mashed ruin.

He brings a cheese board next, and I reach for it instinctively. The curved two-prong tip of the cheese knife glints under the strip light overhead.

I take a glug of the wine, and my head swims. I drink again, and his voice grows distant.

There are crumbs from paper-thin crackers hanging in the corners of his mouth, and he's saying: "Gwen got fired. She got a little too comfortable with the company credit card."

"I'm going to leave, and who the fuck is Gwen?"

He continues his tirade, telling me how people don't want to work anymore and how everyone expects something for nothing.

The wine rushes through my veins as I stand up and fold the napkin back on the table, take my jacket from the back of the chair and sling my arms into the sleeves. My date barely looks up as he chews off the brie's rind and asks if the Stilton looks too blue.

He does not react when I walk the length of the table. The cheese knife is clenched in my hand.

It is solid silver, and I'll be taking it when I'm done.

The door is in view, right behind him and off to the right, just past the kitchen area where the server has disappeared.

Finally, as I tower above him, I tell my most disappointing date, "Can't beat good company. Good conversation." He shuffles his body in the rusty chair made of repurposed piping, perhaps from some water plant built before the second World War.

Two things happen in the following seconds: I notice how easily the gentle serration of a silver cheese knife bites through the mass of flesh in a man's neck; he expects an answer to his question. "Why?"

Eyes wide, blood bubbling through the makeshift maw I've created in the flaccid skin of his aging neck. "Why?" His voice is a hushed whisper, the cut has taken out a portion of the vocal cords.

I want to say something quippy, something quick-witted and smart that will make me feel like I'm in a movie, like from the posters that adorn every wall of the minimalist rustic living area built from chunks of the Berlin Wall or marble from Olympus or the last limestone pillars of Atlantis; whatever fairy tale shit he was sold to con him into this bygone interior.

I wipe the knife on his Hugo Boss dress slacks before the blood can drip into his lap, and I place the knife in the inside pocket of my jacket, its forked tongue making a snag in the fabric.

As I head for the exit, the server appears in the doorway. His eyes widen into two huge luminous moons as he views the corpse slumping further down in the uncomfortable chair, blood saturating the Calvin Klein and the Dolce & Gabbana beneath it. He retreats back into the kitchen, and the door swings comedically, all but a server-shaped hole in the atmosphere where he once existed.

I reach the exit, and notice even the door is a joke, a gargantuan sliding contraption salvaged from the empty husk of a barn.

"Because you chew like a fucking animal."

There is no loss when someone like him is gone from the world. I consider it doing my civic duty, taking out the trash. The world's a better place without him, and I'm satisfied with how it went, though I can feel in my gut it was over too soon. And I let him off too easily.

I take the elevator to the deserted lobby and leave through the revolving, gold-plated front door. I don't care about the hidden security cameras that might be recording me or the distant sound of sirens that carry on the night air. I feel nothing.

I don't care. But I think, *this is New York*.

Let them try and find me: the "Real Estate" guy; the one whose name he never asked; the one who doesn't exist outside of this moment. Nothing but a stolen silver cheese knife, and the word of a server who never once looked me in the eye, to prove I'd ever been there .

And honestly if I had to admit to why I did it, why I

took the time and effort to rid the world of one more man-sized human vacuum ....

It was the signed poster; what a fucking poser. Which is an ironic thought coming from someone who's whole life is a piece of performance art, but I never said I was rational.

I walk a few streets over, hail a cab, and travel the distance back to Brooklyn in silence, making it home in a record thirty-seven minutes. I'm wearing a surgical mask even though no one seems to give a shit about the miasma of deadly disease mutating throughout the city, so my face is covered in darkness and fabric, and I dismount the taxi a five-minute walk from my front door.

When I crawl into bed, I sleep an uninterrupted nine hours, as if nothing had happened at all. I don't regret a thing.

And I note, when I get the chance, I need to find a new gym.

CHAPTER TWO

THERE'S A KNIFE IN MY pocket. I forget about it until I sling my jacket back on. Its sharp edges grate too close for comfort to my nipple through the fine fabric of my button-down, and I dread to think of what the inside lining looks like after stashing a hastily cleaned murder weapon there for the past twelve hours. My eye starts to twitch as I lift it out, hear it peel away from the silk lining, and see the imprint of the accent fabric's pattern rendered in rusty brown upon the blade. It's the Bayeux tapestry printed on Excalibur in gore by Vlad the Impaler. In a way, it's art. It's *my* art.

The secret is to spread out the victims. It's *Law & Order* 101; watch any crime show, and they'll specify the importance of patterns in finding a serial killer. No patterns—*Ipso facto,* no serial killer. Basic math with a side of psychology. New York is gargantuan, but if I knocked off too many of these guys in the same vicinity, the police wall map, with its interconnecting strings, would show a radius of a mile around my house. It'd make it too easy to find me, and thus far, they have yet to come close, not even a phone call. And it's all down to my lack of planning.

I pick victims on the Upper East Side, Queens, Hell's Kitchen, Staten Island one week, and the Bronx the next. I'm sporadic with timing. Change my MO when I can, some during the day, some in the morning, or some at night. My weapon is one of convenience, a garrote made from a shoelace, an ice pick like Sharon Stone, or anything sharp, blunt, ridged, or heavy I can lay my hands on. And I make no plans ahead of time. It looks random, just a series of unfortunate murders in a city notorious for such things, and it seems like that because, in effect, it is. My natural preference is blood; more is better, so opening an artery or creating a cavernous well in the back of a bulbous skull is what I crave.

I stash the cheese knife in the kitchen drawer next to the potato peeler and the masher that always stops the drawer from closing smoothly. It doesn't belong there, but I'll take it and put it where it needs to go later, stow it in the crawl space with the other tokens and trophies, under the floorboards of a coat closet that never gets opened except for that very purpose. It'll join all the other souvenirs I've gathered over the years, too many to count, but each with a memory I can feel as I hold it. Weaponry of all calibers, knives and garrotes, blunt instruments, and tiny trinkets of religious or personal significance, all sheafed in plastic and cataloged beneath the floorboards where I never let dust gather.

Hastily, I head out the door and get in the car, a mid-sized Subaru in gunmetal gray, ready for work. In my mind, I sound a mantra, over and over, ready to put on the mask that makes me appear like anyone else. I fake my script for any pleasantries that might be required, all the *Hi*'s and *How are you*'s that let me slide in and out without making too much of an impression on the people in my radius. My stomach sloshes with grapefruit segments, jelly toast, and coffee, churning and squelching audibly as I throw my satchel onto the passenger seat and buckle myself in.

I'm on the bridge in rush hour, fighting to switch lanes but keeping my cool as much as possible. I could slash up a road traffic violator with such glee that they'd be pulling ribbons of skin from the East River for decades afterward. I'm awash in a sea of vehicular rage as I edge my way, inch by inch, across the bridge.

Nearly an hour later, I arrive at the office, park in the underground garage and take the elevator to the eleventh floor. Speckman & Wise, Graphic Design Agency, is open for all your graphic needs.

Inside the backmost office, I take my jacket off and sling it over the back of the chair. In doing so, I notice a spot of blood on the cuff, dried purple, barely visible against the dark fabric. And I think, *fuck*, because why did I put my jacket on before killing that asshole? I guess it was for the smooth exit. To be that guy who can just sweep away, Bond-Style from a dark situation with a quip and a spring in his step, Leonardo DiCaprio in *Catch Me If You Can*, a hybristophilic pin-up for the new generation, but only in my own head.

Wearing this jacket the night after it adorned my body on one of my kills was a bad idea, and I chided myself for being careless. The jacket is, however, the perfect accompaniment to these pants. If I'm honest with myself, there is a thrill to carrying around a clue only you know about from a crime committed anonymously. And as aggravated as I am about the damage to the outerwear, I breathe, calm myself and settle. It plagues me.

It won't do to leave it, and I make a note to take it to the dry cleaners on the way out of the office. There is this Russian dry-cleaning place down the block that doesn't ask questions, though this tiny splotch will barely raise an eyebrow. I once had them get arterial spray out of cashmere, and they did it with a smile.

Before I take my seat for the morning, I scrawl a reminder onto a post-it and stick it above the surrounding desktop screen where I won't be able to miss it on my way back out the door when the masquerade of daily life is all curtains.

I'm sat in a swivel chair within minutes, sans jacket with the artistic blood stains, typing the same password I use for everything into a state-of-the-art Mac computer so advanced that it could send an army to space while lagging from a phishing virus acquired via porn. The screen is this arced monstrosity that takes up the entire back length of the desk and I can't see past it without craning my neck over it .

I have three unread emails, none of which are urgent or require even opening presently, so I take an iPad from my satchel and start scrawling some rough images. I draw the guy from last night, his neck slashed wide like a screaming mouth, draw the flash of white cartilage where I exposed his Adam's apple, shade in the negative space around his ruined vocal cords, like guitar strings strumming with sound. It's a comic book sketch, and I add a speech bubble coming from the open wound that says: *You're not my usual type*. It makes me laugh.

I'm frantically adding blood spatter that didn't happen to add emphasis, to make the picture frenetic, to make it feel more horrific. The honest truth was the night was underwhelming. As soon as I woke up this morning, I had the itch to kill again. It comes and goes, but when it comes, it comes hard, and I can feel it starting to build again, this pang in my gut that feels like longing, that feels like falling in love. It's the first eye contact in a crowded room or the moment you realize the depths of your commonality. It's fear and longing tied together in a gift bag, ready to hand over.

When it gets like this, everyone starts to look appetizing: the guy at the reception desk on the mail run; the nerd with the specs in the office next door; the guy at the Spanish bodega where I buy vodka and toilet paper, and cigarettes on the days I decide I want to be a smoker. All of them could take the edge off in one way or another, but I have to reel it in, have to conserve some enthusiasm until the dead guy from last night is last week's news.

Time flies as I shade the negative space, add flurries of red, shadow the quote with a faded grey, and before I know it, it's midday.

Lunch is sushi from Sushi Yasaka on 72nd; Donburi, Kinmedai, Miso soup and a seltzer. It would be quicker and cheaper to order from Sushi Seki in Times Square, but I once got food poisoning from a bad salmon roll, and it's not tasted the same since. The delivery guy arrives with my lunch, sweating, in shorts and a tight-fitting muscle tee, and sets the brown bag down in front of me.

There's a letter opener in the drawer tucked to the right beneath the glass surface, and I'm curious to know what delivery guy would look like gutted from gullet to groin, his entrails spilling out like so much meat, blood cascading on the high shine of the tabletop pane. I can smell the fresh scent of delivery guy's sweat in the air. I think about cranking one out where I sit, the door still open into the communal space beyond, delivery guy looking down at me with his vacant blush. I think about blowing my load all over the shared keyboard and computer screen and the next guy in here covering his fingertips in my DNA while eating a sub from the crummy deli across the street.

I tip him twenty as an apology for the graphic death method I envision for him. Our fingertips connect in a second of electric contact that ends before I'm ready to let it. He thanks me with a smile like he's never had a tip before, and I'm hard as rock beneath the desk. He waves goodbye and leaves, but the thrill remains.

My arousal dies by the time it takes me to answer the three emails, plus that two that have arrived in the meantime. Asides from the graphic death sketch of last nights failed first date and an almost surgically precise daydream of how to perform a living autopsy on a delivery guy, I've achieved nothing of note all day.

And at a quarter to four, my cell starts to buzz in my pocket, an unknown number from somewhere in the city. I rarely answer unknown numbers, but the boredom is overwhelming. My mind is wrought with visions of evisceration and decapitation, vivisection and exsanguination, and I can't focus on the little work I have to do. The day is as good as done, and I figure, *what the hell*, so I answer it.

I say: "Mallory," and grimace. I hate how cornfed my voice sounds with a cell phone pressed to my ear, like some *aww shucks* southern fuck, chewing on a sheaf of wheat.

The muffled voice of the woman on the call says: "Mister Mallory, this is Nurse Nevins from Bellevue Emergency. Can I please confirm this is Jacob Duncan Mallory, cell number…" and she lists off my number, verbatim.

"That's me," I say in that good ol' boy drawl. "What can I do for you?"

The nurse clears her throat and says: "We've had an admission that has you listed as their emergency contact."

"Oh yeah? Can you tell me who it is?" As far as I'm aware, I've never been asked to be listed as an emergency contact for anyone, so this is news to me.

She replies with a sigh, "The young man has requested we not give his details at this point. We are asking that you come down to Bellview. He is high risk, and he needs to be released to someone before he can leave. I'm sorry I can't share more information."

They had me at *young man*. The day just started looking up.

And on the way to the hospital, I'm thinking I don't know anyone in the city well enough to be relied on like this. I haven't got family here, no friends to speak of. Only casual acquaintances related to work and even then, I'd be hard pressed to name a single person I was close enough to that would ever trust me like this.

I drive through the mild traffic, switching and swapping lanes, to navigate my way to 1st Avenue. I know the area well, have killed as many as four people in and around Kips Bay, and as I locate the hospital, I'm distracted trying to conjure the faces of the victims and their circumstances scattered across this part of Manhattan. Some I remember well, and some illude me; it's not always a memorable experience by any stretch of the imagination. The memory and the blood are tied together, inseparable in how much of my memory they take up.

I pull into the parking lot, the butterflies in my stomach feel more like bats. It's that first date feeling, but with the added trepidation of the blind date.

Belleview is an aching old excrescence, a red brick Highrise with old wrought iron front gates emblazoned with the hospital name. I walk for nearly ten minutes to find the right entrance and before long, I find myself in the emergency room. Inside the hospital, it's a standard interior, complete with blinding strip lights and the smell of antiseptic with the undertones of human rot. It's surprisingly busy for a weekday afternoon, and I'm lost in a sea of bleeding, crying and agitated patients, all boiling into a rage at the time it's taking to get seen by a doctor, to be stitched up, or medicated and sent on their way.

I grab a mask on my way in, cover my face quickly to guard from all the hacking and coughing and potentially transmissible fluids flying around the place. You'd think I wouldn't care, given my extracurricular activities, but on the whole, I'm fairly germaphobic. Three shots of hand sanitizer and I find my way to the reception. There's mellow elevator music being piped through an overhead system, trying to lull the cattle, trying to create an atmosphere of calm where no calm is found.

A black nurse in rainbow scrubs asks: "Can I help you, honey?" as I rub my hands together, the strong vodka scent making its way to evaporation towards my cloth-covered nose or absorption into the skin of my hands.

"I had a call," I say, subconsciously smiling behind the mask. "Nurse Nevin?"

She says: "Can I take your name?" so I let her have it.

Within the minute, Nevin arrives at the desk, a ball of static fueled by caffeine and kinetic energy, and I'm being led behind a curtain, through a corridor to where the beds are laid out in various divisions, sets of six in each partition, all facing inwards like anyone would want to spend their infirmed days staring at other sickly people. Nevin is short and strong, with an air of confidence radiating off her compact five-foot-three stature. She walks without needing to see, looking behind herself blindly to check I'm keeping pace. As I follow her quick steps, shortening my own to avoid crashing into the back of her, she's telling me: "He stumbled in here this afternoon. It was a suicide attempt, so when you see him, he might be a bit of a mess."

She still hasn't told me who *he* is.

We take a right and then a left and we are in the bowels of the hospital department, where the rooms are more sporadic, the lights are dimmer, the presence of New York's finest seems to have increased, despite the lack of motion or noise or need.

She says: "He's restrained, but we had to do it around the feet. The wrists aren't up to anything until he heals a bit."

I cock an eyebrow and she smiles with her eyes, crinkling above the white strip at the top of her mask. "Don't worry, I don't think he's dangerous. We just couldn't risk him leaving before the attending doctor had given us the go ahead and we had his emergency contact to release him to."

I don't know why I'm here other than morbid curiosity. Even if I know this mysterious *he,* it's not like I'd care enough to babysit the basket case. As time has passed it has become too late to ask who this person is, and the bats in my stomach are flocking violently upwards because I know there's no way I'm taking this guy out of here with me.

So, I ask: "What exactly do you need me to do?"

Nurse Nevin turns to me and puts her hands on her hips. "Suicide watch, 72 hours and if he's fine then you can do what you like."

She clears the final corner into his room, and I follow behind her, clueless, but now the beneficiary of a suicide flight risk, one with cut up wrists and bound to a gurney by his feet.

I take an antiseptic breath through blue fibers. This is not the way I intended my day to go.

But still, I think.

Worst comes to worse, I can get a kill in and be home in time for dinner.

I look down at the purple splotch of blood on my jacket sleeve. Maybe I'll need to burn the jacket after all. I step into the room behind Nevin, and I stop and gaze in wonder.

There *he* is, all pitiful and vulnerable, unconscious, and unprepared. And he's perfect.

Aww shucks.

CHAPTER THREE

THE NAME ON HIS CHART says *Nathan McGuire*. I've never seen him before in my life. He's like me, the kind of guy you could fail to notice on the street, unremarkable outside the situation, just another guy until you notice the details. He's a blank canvas, and one I'm aching to spray paint red like a Banksy without the stencils.

He's strapped to the bed by his ankles with these greasy-looking peach bindings you see in every movie about a psych ward ever made. It's *Cuckoo's Nest*, it's *Devil's Advocate*. His brown cord pants are rolled up to the knees exposing his white-socked feed and a healthy thatch of dark leg hair. Like an animal, drool starts to flood my mouth, hungry for what comes next though I can't conjure the image in my head.

I look him over like you'd view something in the chiller at the grocery, weighing up the options, seeing if I'm willing to buy. He's mid-twenties, just shy of six feet from what I can tell. His skin is the pallid color of anemia, and his face is fixed in a sleeping sedation, covered with a mop of unruly brown hair emerging from beneath a drawn red hood.

The red riding hood similarity is jarring. I could be the wolf, right? I run my tongue across my teeth. *All the better to eat you with.*

He's attractive and younger than my usual type, but I'm not looking to date him. No, it's his vulnerability that appeals. Something about him speaks to me in a way nothing has before. He has 'victim' written all over him, his thin, sinewy body coiled up tight, like in sleep he thinks he can be protected.

And I know, as I watch this sleeping stranger, I know that if he comes to and accepts my offer to break him out of here, I will kill him and take my time doing it. I could tear him limb from limb and have his blood flowing out in torrents of red ruin. Hell, in 72 hours, I could flay all the skin from his body and not break a sweat. The options are endless, but I make no move to plan this out.

Even with the change of acquisition, planning is off the table. Let the games begin.

I can't be the same nonchalant guy who quips to the twitching body of a dying socialite. I have to be on my game. The guy in the bed doesn't stir, but something dark and primal stirs in me. And I'm ready.

His stitched wrists are bound in white bandages peeking from the edges of chewed, red sleeves. I imagine that when all is said and done, I'll open those wounds again, ping the stitches one by one with a sharp blade, and let him bleed out in these lush rivers of red all over the hardwood.

And I'll drop his body in the Hudson, let him wash ashore or be eaten by the fish, the tragic end of a suicidal man to cover the indescribable brutality wrought upon him by the stranger he invited into his life.

Nurse Nevin hands me a Ziploc bag of his belongings: a cell phone straight out of 2007, a kids Velcro wallet, some keys, some Juicy Fruit gum, and an antique-looking wristwatch he won't be able to wear again, maybe ever. And she says: "Let him rest for now," lowering her voice to a whisper so as not to rouse him. She says: "If you're happy to wait a while, just take a seat, and when he wakes up, we can start the paperwork."

And so, I sit in this sticky, high-backed hospital chair beside his bed with this plastic bag of personals I plan to root through as soon as the nurse leaves us in peace, my hands itching to begin my game.

She plumps the cushions behind his head, gives another masked smile with just her eyes, and vacates the small room, closing the door behind her. I open the bag and appraise Nathan McGuire, my next victim.

His cellphone is password protected, so that's a no-go. I think about trying his unconscious thumbprint but don't want to wake him before I get my lay of who this kid is under the hood, under the bandages, and the look of complete innocence struck through with the insane self-hatred in what he's done to himself.

His wallet is all I have to give me answers, so I scoop it out of the bag and set the rest of the contents on the floor. His license provides the introduction I need: Nathan McGuire. His home address is some shithole in Hoboken, and he turned twenty-seven a couple months ago. In his driver's license photo, there's light in his eyes, the hint of a smile; he doesn't look desperate enough to take a blade to major veins and arteries. This is not the same kid sedated in the bed at my side. His hair is shorter in the picture, and he looks healthier—his skin has the hint of a blush, and his face is rounder. Then I look at him now. Hard times, kid.

I place the little plastic card back in the designated slot in his wallet and pull out the rest of the contents.

And there, on top, is my business card. The edges of the weathered paper folded like the last read page of a paperback novel. It makes me wonder how many times his fingers have touched my name and why this card, in particular, was one he's held onto. It's all you'd need to fill out a form; my name, place of work, address of my office, and contact number of both the front desk and the switchboard that transfers you to my cell. Even in this condition, the card is a work of art, the thickness of the paper and the gentle render of the font screaming the quality that went into producing it, the finish ethereal and a gift beneath the fingertips. I caress the card the way I imagine he has done, and the feeling of silk beneath my skin feels calming. Maybe that's all there is to it.

Seeing my card in there makes no sense, but given the situation, you have to figure he just needed a name for the form, and one on a found business card is just as good as any. I imagine he thought a stranger would take pity on him if he ever needed to use it, would drop him home, and make sure he's alright. If any other person's card had sat where mine did in his wallet, the kid might make it out of this in better shape than I found him. But not Nathan McGuire, not today.

If only he had known when he picked up the card what kind of situation he was courting, of who was at the other end of this thread he was pulling despite knowing nothing of what he was reeling in.

I place the wallet back in the plastic baggy, set it on the edge of the bed, and wait. A clock on the wall loudly ticks, and I time my breaths to meet the intervals. Breathe in. Breathe out.

Eventually, he stirs in the bed beside me, and slowly, beneath the curtain of hair and the blood-red hood, he opens his eyes.

And I smile. *Hello, Nathan McGuire,* my thoughts whisper. *I'm the last person who's ever going to see you alive.*

THE SKY IS STARTING TO darken as we arrive in Brooklyn, pull the car up onto the streetside parking spot outside my apartment, and get out. There's a chill in the air that is coming earlier each day. The further from fall we get, the closer to the New Year.

In the time it took to sign Nathan out, discuss his situation with his physician, and sign the papers needed to get him this far, he hasn't spoken a word to me. In turn, I haven't stopped talking, asking relentless question after question that he's refused to answer, just staring idly out the window, watching the skyline pass us by. At times, I wondered if it wouldn't have been easier just to open the door on the bridge and chuck him out into the river, but occasionally he'd turn to look at me, and I'd get that thrill of possibility jolting through my body.

I know where he lives, and we've passed the turn-off to get there miles back, and I asked: "Do you need to get anything from your place?"

Nathan McGuire stayed mute and didn't answer, and I was glad for his silence, an acquiescence that he belonged to me.

And I asked him: "Are you in any pain?" and all he did was rattle the bottle of painkillers he'd been prescribed when the doctor had palmed him off to me without so much as a check of my identification, the only concern the hospital had been getting this guy out the door and the next bleeding victim into the void where he once occupied a hospital bed.

It's all gone too smoothly, but I try not to question it. Nathan gets out of the car and shuts the door behind him.

I think, *what now?*

And he starts walking towards the doors to my apartment building, holding this flopping plastic baggy in one bound hand, the other hanging at his side like so much dead weight. And I watch this broken kid just wander into the path of danger.

The apartment building is this new build, three-story walk-up with students in the basement and some absent second homeowners taking the middle unit. Mine is the top. It's the ideal setup. Throughout any given year, I only worry about the downstairs tenants during the summer months. For the rest of the year, I could commit mass murder, and the drunk and stoned academics in the subterranean apartment would be none the wise.

We walk the two flights up to my front door, and through the slight heft in his baggy cords, I notice how he moves his round ass as he walks, swaying and swinging in this seductive side-to-side motion. I stare, and he doesn't look back. And I lick my lips. We arrive at the front door, and I snake my arm around him to unlock the door, pressing him between my body and the wooden paneling. He looks at me out of the side of his eye and I see a smile. He smells like perspiration and some knockoff body spray by some second-rate sports brand. It's alluring, nonetheless. I open the door, and, together, we step inside, into the small foyer. Beyond that is the kitchen, open plan and splaying into the lounge area.

My voice turns the lights on. Everything has a clinical aesthetic clinging to it, white high gloss and chrome everything, a black monochrome color scheme, and pale, dappled walls pristine as the day they were painted. The fridge looks like a body locker and there are kitchen gadgets on the worksurfaces that do things like knead dough or grind meat, which have never been used. The whole room is Ikea chic, supplemented with the homeware section of the Sears catalog. Take that, and make it lifeless, sterile, and easy to identify errant blood spatters. He walks around the chrome kitchen island that swallows the bulk of the room and runs his hand across the countertop.

Looking at this place through a stranger's eyes, I start to see what it looks like, like a morgue you could live in. But, as I lay my keys down on the kitchen counter, Nathan turns and looks at me, properly looking me in the eye for the first time since he woke up.

And he says: "Nice place."

His voice is deep and buttery, but with that dry hitch you get when you smoke too much, too young. His lips curl into this half smile with a hint of warmth, and I feel my face grow warm.

I try and play it straight, to play the host, and say: "Make yourself at home", and he wanders off out of the kitchen and into the lounge area beyond. The lights come up when he enters the room. They are automated and motion censored and are built into the preset, curated mode for the evenings, with a dulled burnt-orange hue to help soften the edges of the frosty aesthetic.

I say: "Fire on," and flames burst behind sheet glass built into the wall, warming the space up instantly. I say: "Main screen on," and the TV comes alive with a Doppler dot that expands into 4k ultra vision with Dolby surround singing its activation.

I watch from the doorway as he takes everything in, the minimalist lack of charm, the technological wonders that these days only a poor kid could appreciate, the lack of any personality.

I say: "Have a seat."

He sits, following orders like a dog. That's what he reminds me of, sinking back into my couch, dwarfed by oversized grey cushions built for comfort; he looks like a rescue dog liberated from the pound.

I ask him: "Have you been to Brooklyn much?" He just shakes his head.

And I ask him: "Is there anyone I can call for you? Like, a friend or something?" and he looks lost, and sad, and I fight that feeling in between my dick and my asshole that's falling head over heels for how utterly fucking damaged he looks.

I don't know what I'm doing with this kid, but I need at least the night to figure it out. The apartment is decked with state-of-the-art security, coded and camera surveillance, so he won't be able to leave without my being alerted. So, I decide he stays the night, I'll get him settled in, build him up to make it all the more devastating when I break him down.

And I sit in a matching gray armchair, and I wait. And I ask him: "So tell me about yourself." And I use this light tone like the kind you might use talking to a child or an old person sitting in a puddle of piss.

The silence is stifling, and within seconds he moves to break it by opening his mouth, but he can't find the words. The muted TV screen casts a multicolored glow across his pale face.

And I say: "It's okay if you don't want to talk. You're safe here." The lie feels cruel, and what's crueler is that I like it.

He says, "I'm sorry, this is weird," and I look at him but don't respond. Not straight away. I feel this intense need to know what's going on here, from his perspective, through this unassuming kid's lost, deer-in-the-headlights eyes. From my point of view, I'm playing with my food, but I want to know what he thinks he's walked into with me, here in this remote part of Brooklyn with neighbors that can't hear you scream.

I lean back and cross my legs like a silent therapist, some altruistic sage-type sent to guide him. He had my card and knew I'm a graphics expert, yet I want him to think of me as a mentor. Or a master.

The silence breaks into pieces once more when he says, "I didn't have anyone…" looks down and takes a deep breath. "I had your card in my wallet. Picked it up last year after you did that expo appearance in Time Square. And they asked me for a contact and…"

And he pauses again.

I remain quiet, letting him finish, and it's just like I thought. There will be no one to miss him, no one to mourn him. I do not need to rush this at all. This kid is broken in ways I can imagine, and I think of the great pleasure it will give me to convince him I'll fix him, to mend him the way I wish someone had restored me when it might have made a difference.

And I think of how much glee it will give me to take it away again.

He looks so sad, but he's lit with this angelic glow I want to inhale. He is this tragic, beautiful thing; nothing will give me greater pleasure than destroying it. I can't say I won't enjoy it because I will. This could be my greatest achievement, my pièce de résistance, my magnum opus. I plan to break this kid open like ripe fruit and hollow him out, starting with his skull.

He says: "I don't have any family, and I'm pretty new in the city, so I don't really know anyone." This is a lie, I know. He has a New York driver's license, so unless he recently passed his test, he's a New Yorker through and through. I can hear it in his voice, but I let it slide. The lies won't mean much in a few days, and if he needs to tell them, then what do I care as long as I get what I want?

I keep quiet. I can tell it's driving Nathan mad. And he

gets up and says: "I can go," and looks at me. "I should go," and he makes a move for the way he came out of the lounge and back towards the kitchen.

And I stop him, get up, stand in his path, lay my hands on his arms, warming in that red riding hood, and I say: "You can stay. I don't want you to be alone."

I feel the tension in his arms relax in my hands. I feel the burden of uncertainty unravels from within him. Tonight, I know, I will get him to relax. I will provide safety and a good place to stay. Tomorrow can wait.

"Can I get you a drink?" I move towards the kitchen, the light sensor triggering as I enter the room.

"You got a beer?"

I sneer. "In this house," I say, grabbing a Chateau Neuf du Pape from the beneath-the-counter wine rack, "we drink the good stuff".

I take two glasses suspended downwards by their stems from their home beneath a high cupboard and open the drawer to find a bottle opener.

The cheese knife of last night's slaughter glares back at me, it's teeth still brown with the ichor from the slain idiot's neck, and I remind myself I have to file that away in the right way, list and label and let it take its place in my collection with the rest of the stolen trophies of murders past.

I wonder what trophy I'll take from the kid.

I generously fill the glasses, and I hold one out to him as he moves towards me, leaning into the countertop to support him as he grabs the crystal stem. A toast to his last supper. A fine last meal to come.

I swill the glass, let the ruby liquid aerate, and pull its scents through my nose. It's all an act. I don't know what

I smell, and I have no idea what I'm supposed to get from this. I take a gentle pull from the glass and roll the fluid in my mouth with the wet slurping sound I've seen on TV, and I close my eyes and groan in pleasure. It serves no purpose but points me in the right light. I seem older and wiser, have life experience and skills, and am a role model, someone to feel safe with. That's what I need him to see in me.

When I open my eyes, he watches me taste the wine, before chewing on his bottom lip, the hint of a flush in his pale white cheeks.

I lick my lips and say: "That's not bad," like I would know what bad tasted like. It's a mid-price red, and I only know about reds when they don't taste right. This tastes just fine like a good red always does when I drink it.

I nod, and he repeats the charade, swirling and sniffing and slurping and swilling, and then matches the final swallow with a moan.

It's a dance, but something about that moan seduces me. Nathan is playing a good game. I grab the bottle with my spare hand, lead him back to the lounge, and let him settle in for the night, snuggle in the warm, functional cushions, and let his guard fall.

I let him choose the movie we watch, pick what food we order and pay for it, collect it from the door, and present it with plates and paper napkins.

Gradually I see his body relax, and his long legs curl up into the couch, a smile crossing his face as he laughs at the scenes on the television.

And I watch as he becomes less and less aware of the danger he's in.

CHAPTER FOUR

WHEN I'M POURING HIS GLASS from the second bottle, I notice that he's fiddling with the sleeves of his sweater, pulled down over his fists, bunched in clenched hands. With the dim light, it's hard to see, but once I notice, there's no unseeing it; there is dried blood snaking its way all up the inner arm, camouflaged against the red of the cotton. Red on red under orange light, and I don't blame myself for missing it, but now that I see it, it bothers me more and more.

Where the blood has pooled up to his elbow, the fabric has hardened and doesn't move or bend like cotton. I've intimately studied how blood works and drawn the effects in each of my sick sketches, and now I see it, it's hard to ignore. I'm guessing it's carnage under that protective cloak of red fabric.

He's had the hooded sweater on the whole time I've been with him, the front zipped right up under his chin. At the base of his brown pants, darker patches rimmed around the bottom as if he's been walking in fresh rainwater, but they are bone dry.

I can picture in my mind this broken guy on a bathroom floor, bleeding out from his wrists, helpless and alone, panicking with regret. It's an odd sensation, but I feel for him, not so much sorrow as pity. If this all works out, I'll see a repeat performance of what should have been his swan song.

While he lifts the stem of the freshly poured wine, bunched in his sweater-clad fist, I get up and walk to my bedroom. He is slenderer and shorter than me, but when it comes to workout clothes, everything is elasticated and has drawstrings. I find him something old from within my drawers, something I won't miss but will have to remove from him before the final act of this play takes place. I choose old joggers and an oversized tee, and some promotional zip-up sweater I got from some event I was forced to attend. If memory serves me right, I killed the guy who gave it to me—crushed his skull in the sliding side doors of his shitty off-white van—for no other reason than a distaste for the garish printed decal on the front of the sweater.

Nathan is laughing, lulled by wine and the warmth of the fire. When I hand him the small pile of clean clothes. he gives me a puzzled expression. The furrow in his brow is deep, a dark ridge in the pristine white skin of his forehead, and for a second, I'm just staring at it, gawping at the magical crevice that seems to crack in the porcelain of his face. It seems like an hour of appraising, but in reality, it's just a second.

And I say: "I figured you could use a change of clothes. Those look…," and I eye him up and down, or as close as

I can from his seated position on the couch. "…like they should be burned." I smile. I'm used to burning clothes when necessary. I don't tell him this.

He takes the pile from my hands and stands up. I expect him to move to somewhere more private, but he starts to undress in front of me with no thought for modesty. There's no room for modesty when I've seen him in a vulnerable condition at the hospital and sat beside him while he slept off a sedative to stem the pain from the gashes in his wrists.

He unzips the hooded sweater and peels it off, the sleeves audibly stripping away from his skin where remnants of spilled blood have adhered to the fabric. Beneath that, he wears a white t-shirt, and without the sweater to cover it, he looks like a murder victim, slashes and pools of blood seeped down and spray painted across his torso, the thin fabric almost translucent where it's tacked itself to the pale skin on his body. I stare in silence and awe as he reveals the road map of what he went through before the hospital before they stitched up his wrists and paused his demise.

He places the sweater on the coffee table; it's dry, so nothing will transfer, though I make a mental note to clean it well when all is said and done. He leaves his t-shirt and unbuttons his long pants, letting them slide past the pale fabric of his boxers, down long muscular legs, dark hair emerging beneath his underwear, and never relenting until it meets the crown of his socks. He removes everything from his pockets before dumping them on the coffee table.

He spares a second to glance at me before he removes the t-shirt, slowly, untacking it gently from where it is bound to his skin and the hair on his chest and stomach. It joins the rest on the coffee table.

There are a few errant splotches of blood on his boxers, and when he looks down and notices, he pulls them off and stands before me, naked, lean, and muscular, almost undulating with this emanating sense of masculinity that is intoxicating to behold. There is something innately beautiful about him, like some marble statue of the figures of ancient Greece, of Adonis in perfection, Narcissus before his mirror, but something weighted, more like Sisyphus and his boulder; Atlas holding up the weight of the world.

Our eyes meet, and he bites his lip coyly and asks: "Don't suppose you got any spare boxers?" And I'm forced to step away from the show to retrieve a pair. When I return, he's exhibiting a modicum of modesty, his hand over his genitals, large and thick behind his hand, before using that same hand to take the underwear from me.

A simple exchange, the gentlest touch, yet something is happening to me. And I'm not alone in this; it looks like there's blood rushing elsewhere, just a little, the start of arousal playing along the lines of Nathan's thick cock.

And he dresses quickly: boxers, t-shirt, joggers, and sweater. Then he picks up his wine and takes a swig, and I'm rendered momentarily speechless. And I am never without words.

I pick up his discarded clothes and start to fold them.

He says: "You don't have to worry about those. If you're happy for me to keep these on, then they can go in the trash. Just…" and he pauses. "Can you keep the hoody? It was my… never mind." And he tries again. "It's important."

I think of my jacket, the one I'd worn the night before while on my date in TriBeCa, and the small amount of my date's arterial blood on it and say: "I have to take a jacket to the dry cleaner tomorrow. I can get it cleaned if you like?"

I won't, of course. The significant meaning of this item of clothing means it will stay, bloodied and unwashed, as my trophy of this kill, pre-emptive but all the more sentimental.

And he smiles, nods. "That would be nice."

His brazen exhibitionism has been tampered with by the comfort of the oversized workout clothes, and he's back to being boyish, coy, and timid. It's almost like an act, but I can't think of a reason for what he might want to gain from my approval of his form.

I prefer the more outlandish version. And I think, *might have to get Nathan out of his clothes again before I'm done with him.* My cock throbs with the thought; he's not my type, not really. I tend to like them older. It's easier to snuff out a life if it's longer, more likely riddled with wrongs that need righting. I can sleep at night if I think that way, but this guy is barely an adult, despite how his body has blossomed into something strong and sensual.

And my mind takes off down these avenues of sub-thought, and I think about the hair that coats his body, what it would feel like to run my fingers through it, to take a fistful of his scalp in my hand and clench as I run my tongue down the softness of his pale skin.

I grab my wine glass, sit back in the armchair and cross my legs to cover my stiffening cock, to mask my arousal. It would be careless of me to try and fuck him, no matter how good it might feel. I would be leading forensics to my door if I did everything I wanted to do to him before making him the latest addition to my long list of victims.

And for some reason, I start to feel nervous, the way you're meant to on a first date; the anticipation, the expectation, they create this tingle in my guts that I've only ever found previously in the wake of a good killing, when the blood is drying, or the skin is turning blue. It's nowhere near as palpable, and it'll never be enough, but I'm shocked by the feeling, and it's throwing me off my game.

I start trying to impress the guy and lie about what I've done. I tell him I met Abigail Breslin at La Bernardin, Sandra Bernhardt on Broadway, Benicio Del Toro in the Meat Packing District at a party we were both invited to. I am one signed movie poster away from being the kind of person I revel in killing, making me feel sick. The words sound wrong coming out of my mouth; honestly, I have no idea who Sandra Bernhardt is and wouldn't be able to pick Del Toro out of a lineup.

And he tells me he's from Cleveland and was a theatre major before he came to New York to make it big. It's a tale as old as time, and I realize no one would miss this guy if I disappeared for good. And I start to see shades of myself there, the guy no one sees, a ghost who can walk in and walk out, and no one ever truly notices, a failed day player in the performance of New York.

And my heart almost aches for him and for myself, to be the invisible person without anything to lose. He makes me see a side of myself I never consider, and it hurts. It's lonely, and I don't feel like being alone.

The mood shifts as I sit beside him on the couch, pour him another drink, and ask him the asinine questions you ask on a date, the ones I never get to ask, the ones that would be ignored if I did. I say: "Have you ever been to the top of the Chrysler Building?" and I ask: "What's the last play you saw?" and I'm asking: "What books do you love?" and the whole thing is an attempt to make me normal.

I'm just a guy, sitting in front of a guy.

It's one night. I can fake it. What's the harm if I'm only going to kill him later?

He tells me: "I've never even thought about doing all the touristy shit," and he's saying: "I mainly just watch Netflix," and he says: "I don't get much time to read, I'm always working."

I find out he's a catering waiter for a private events company in Williamsburg. He makes enough money to cover rent, bills, his cellphone plan, and eating, but not much else. He says: "I'd never be able to afford a bottle of this stuff," pointing at the wine. "Let alone three. I guess there's good money in graphic design? How'd you get into that? Seems a little boring for a guy like you."

And he's flirting with me, his eyes rarely leaving mine, almost intrusively. I have to blink, turn away, and top up my glass to rip myself from the intensity of his gaze.

The tables have turned from my typical dating plan, and I'm the older, wiser participant, and he's the young ingénue. It's been a while since I considered myself young, but it's easier to pretend when you go for an older man. When they're losing their hair, getting fatter with age, and the booze and smokes start to take their toll on the skin, I feel youngest.

With this kid, I feel like a dinosaur. But all dinosaurs have teeth.

He mutes the movie and moves to face me. His knee rests against mine, and he makes no motion to move it. He asks me: "Are your parents still around?" and he says: "Do you ever feel like you're wasting time?" And he asks: "What would you do if you could do anything in the world you wanted?"

And for the first time on one of these things, I'm engaged, and I'm thinking, despite the river of wine and the nerves and the knowledge that I'm going to kill him any day now. And I can't remember when someone asked me something about myself or truly listened when I replied, even gruesomely. So, I give real, purposeful thought to the answers. Imagine what I would say on a real date with someone like him who is trying to listen to some aging psychopath who didn't realize he was so alone.

But, when all is said and done, to give him the truth is to hand off the power. And that's not something I can afford. My guard stays up, and I reply.

And I answer: "My parents died when I was in college" (they didn't), and I'm telling him: "You get the most out of life by doing the things you love—you only waste time if you're not doing those things," (and I throw up a bit in my mouth), and I tell him: "I'm happy with the way things are going right now," and I wink. It doesn't taste like a lie.

When he answers the same questions, he seems sad. No parents. Time is fleeting. And if he could do anything, he would go back to being a kid, when the world didn't seem like such a shitty place, when he was safe, when he wasn't alone. A tear escapes the corner of his eye, and I lean in and wipe it away with my thumb, and as I pull back, he places a hand over mine, places the wet pad of my thumb into his mouth, and swallows the tear.

CHAPTER FIVE

I PULL BACK, ALMOST IN shock, and Nathan looks bereft. This is not the right time to get drawn into lust-filled soft play with this future cadaver with a perfect smile and a body I want to destroy. This is not the way this needs to play out.

I pull my knee away from his, sink back on the sofa, and polish off the last red in my glass. It tastes like battery acid and bile, and I know I've crossed the line where the previous drink was one too many.

My head is hazy. I know I can't fuck this kid tonight. If I do, then why keep him alive longer? But the thought of ending this too soon, of a cheap night to end this whole charade, doesn't sit right with me. This isn't a movie where we are pressed for time. I want to get into his head before I get into his guts.

With my glass in hand, I walk the short distance to the kitchen, and place it in the empty sink I barely use. And when I'm sure I'm out of Nathan's line of sight, I take a deep breath and feel the headache coming on somewhere near the base of my skull.

And I call out, "You want some water?"

And he replies: "I'm good."

I hear him unmute the movie as I take a water bottle from the fridge, and I know, for me, at least, the night is over.

I wash aspirin down, finishing the enter bottle. I know it'll stave away the hangover as much as anything until the morning when I can fill myself with breakfast.

There is nothing in the house to eat, so it's Post Mates, or we go in search of food together, and the way I like the idea of taking him into the city, of parading him around like a trophy, feels too much like comfort.

I chastise myself again for being week. There are no happy endings for people like me, and he sure as shit won't be getting one.

I walk to the front door, and with my body obscuring it from view, I type the security code into the panel by the lock. I don't typically use it, but I need to know he won't run. I can't take him to bed because I know how that works out, so the best I can do is grab him a blanket and stop picking at this wound before it bleeds.

When I turn to face him, his face is scrunched up in puzzlement, like he has reason to be concerned.

And before he can ask me whatever he wants to, I pre-emptively say: "It'll go off if you open the door. I just need to make sure you don't take off. The nurse said you needed someone with you for at least three days. So, make yourself comfortable."

He rolls his eyes, but there's a playfulness to it.

I grab him another blanket to add to the selection of throws on the back of the couch, figure the myriad cushions surrounding him will serve their purpose, and throw it into his open arms.

"Get some rest," I say, and my voice, slurring under the weight of the wine, is laden with care and warmth. I had no idea I could sound that way, the way you only ever hear from some character on a TV show, some saccharine offering about family values, overcoming the odds and facing fears and demons.

As I walk down the corridor towards my bedroom, I hear his voice, faint behind me, yet rising over a laugh track.

"Thank you," he says. "For all of this."

I close the door.

I DON'T KNOW WHAT TO do with the kid, and I don't plan my kills the way some might. But I know I need to keep him around long enough to make this an epic event. The old guy from last night did little to sate the beast inside me, and I think I may have to kill someone in the meantime, some faceless, nameless nobody, just to prevent my ripping apart Nathan in the next day or two.

I imagine him shucking off his borrowed clothes as before, exposing those long lengths of hair-smattered skin, with the flecks of dried blood pasted to him. I imagine the feel of his mouth around me, the way he wrapped his soft lips around the tip of my thumb. Instinctively I reach down between my legs where my arousal is evident and aching. I fill my mind with Nathan as I take myself in my hand, dry but for the seep of precum from the tip of my cock. I have always been heavy in terms of cum, and I use it to lessen the friction as I move my fist back and forth up and down the length of me.

Nathan's mouth. Nathan's smile. Nathan's body. His eyes. His ass. His cock. His blood.

I grip harder, letting the friction of my uncut cock pleasure my glans as I massage deeply with the palm of my hand, letting it slide its rough friction over my exposed meatus. I start to pant, mouth open, trying to stay calm and silent as I dream of using Nathan's body to my satisfaction. I would take him down with care, prepare him to take every inch of me. I would gaze into his eyes, and I would hold him close.

It's how I envision love must feel.

And when he is there with me, right at the point where our bodies become one and we prepare for the shared release of our intimacy, I would stab him, a sparkling blade that buries in his neck, and watch as the rivers of hot blood spill out over his pale body and onto the sheets below. I would languish and luster in the thick wetness of all that crimson fluid, run my hands through it, and let it drop from his useless hands onto my face and into my hair. He does not fight me, and he cannot move, the haze of his orgasm and the pain and blood loss rendering him without a fight. And I would hold him close until all the breath has left him, so at the end, when I take the last of what he has to give, he is not alone.

I have to stifle my moan, my orgasm muffled beneath the thin draw of my lips. I thrust into my grip as if stabbing into Nathan's body, fierce, reckless motions that bring me to ecstasy. The mess is warm and slick, coating my chest and abs in thick globules of salty spunk, a single thin string making its way to my chin and dribbling down my neck. I use my discarded shirt to mop up the expulsion, feeling its tacky texture mingle into my skin and stick like the residue of glue.

The worst of it will dry on my skin. For now, I sate myself with the few final strokes to rid the softening length of my cock of any remnants of my orgasm, and my eyes grow heavy, my brain stops pounding, and I fall asleep with Nathan's body on my mind, and the room filled with the hot sour aroma of spilled semen.

I can hear the television in the next room but nothing else. The sound is maddening.

CHAPTER SIX

I HADN'T SHUTTERED THE BLINDS, so when the sun rose, its early morning tendrils of acid-hot light burnt wholly onto my face, waking me in a fit of heat and blindness. My head was tender but not as bad as it could have been without the aspirin and the water. It took a second to come around, but when I did, I could hear the sound of the television still blasting outside the door, reminding me of what lay beyond it.

With this new day came the promise of something dark, something fresh to sate a hunger that always burned inside me. I flashback to the night before, the way I imagined myself stabbing violently into the guy's neck as I brought myself to climax. It's enough to harden me again, but I let the thought go. More pressing things ahead that need to be considered.

I let myself slip into the bathroom, keening my ear for any movement beyond, and find nothing. Nathan is inside the apartment somewhere, and judging by his silence, he is still asleep. I check my watch. 6.43 am. He must still be sleeping.

The bathroom provides me sanctuary, to clean myself, to wash the dirt and the cum from my frantic self-flagellation of the night before from my skin and the crusted jizz from my chin that I had forgotten about until the clouded reflection of the bathroom mirror. I clean my teeth, furry with the oxidized flavor of a night on the wine.

I wrap a towel around my waste and exit the bathroom, backlit by a billowing cloud of steam, and find Nathan staring at me, appraising me.

His eyes wander the length of my body, up and down, as if he is committing it to memory. And he excuses himself: "Sorry, just gotta…" and lets himself into the bathroom behind me.

He is awake, and as I dress, I think of what the day can hold, what delicious delights lie before us.

But mostly, I think of breakfast. I could eat.

THERE'S A SHITTY DINER IN Times Square where I go when I've drunk too much. I'll sit in a booth, order the eggs, and flick through a paperback until the bottomless coffee bottoms out. On the way there, I make a detour to the James Hotel, the lot where the Moondance Diner used to stand before they carted it to Wyoming.

As a reformed theatre kid, I figure he'd get a kick out of it, where Larson came up with Tick, Tick, Boom before he commanded the stage with Rent on the night he died. It always struck me as irony; all that hard work just to miss your big break because of some backed-up blood flow in your brain. I think of that more often than I should; what it must be like to tap out before the big finale. Maybe that's what has me in my feels as I give Nathan the sentimental tour of the heart of central New York. We zip down Broadway, back on ourselves through Greenwich, Chelsea, and the Garment District. Traffic is forgiving, and we make good time; we make New York time, which is anything less than infuriating.

It's a long trek from the outer parts of TriBeCa to Times Square, but once those eggs settle in my gut, I know I've made the right choice. Nathan devours bacon and scrambled eggs and sausage like he hasn't eaten in days, despite the pizza we consumed last night. I figure he's one of those people who never gets enough calories and never packs on weight. I don't mind; I'm transfixed watching the rotational spin of his jaw as he masticates burnt-edged bacon and swallows it down that thin, bird-like neck. I imagine my hands wrapped around it, pressing my thumbs in deep, watching his pale pink face turn a grizzly shade of violet.

When we finish eating, I drop the jacket and the red riding hood into the Russian Laundry and sign us up for one of those tourist trips up the One World Observatory, and on the 100th floor, where you can see views out over the entire city, I see him smile, honestly and earnestly for the first time since I found him. The smile reaches his eyes and shows teeth perfect and white, like the boy in the photo on his driver's license. Without even trying, I've met the real kid, one unsullied by life and its horrors.

And it's perfect, the cool winter air brushing against us as we spin to take in the view, standing there mute for an hour to see what we can see from every vantage point the observation deck allows.

He looks happy. And I'm happy he's happy. The height of his happiness is a further way for him to fall. And the more time we spend talking and getting to know each other, the less his guard stays up, the more I can get in, can toy with him the way I've been dying to do.

But I follow the rules, and I don't make plans. With this situation, I have the privilege of time to draw out the process, to make it worth it, one I'll remember, one that will see me through for weeks. I don't plan to cut Nathan open, flay him while he still breathes, or choke his life by crushing that bird-like neck. That's not the way I operate. The spontaneity makes it all the sweeter. This is no different.

He catches me staring at him and asks: "What?"

There's no accusation in it; he just wants to know what I'm thinking, so I offer half the reply. "It's just nice to see you happy."

He stops smiling and looks down, bashful and guilty at the observation. And he doesn't smile like that again.

I BUY HIM A SOFT pretzel from a street kiosk as we walk back to the car from the Russian laundry, the jacket and hoody hooked over my fingers in their clear plastic sheeting, causing a reflective glint of sunshine to bounce on the sidewalk. I watch its hypnotic shine lurch with every step as Nathan takes a mouthful of salted dough and barely chews.

I say: "You can really pack it away, huh? Where does it all go?" And I playfully poke him in his ribs.

He smiles, a humble smile, not one of those happy ones I'd witnessed earlier.

"I eat everything. I'm like, hollow or something."

I laugh.

He chews another bite and swallows. "We didn't have a lot of cash when I was growing up, so we went hungry a lot. I appreciate food a lot more now I can afford to eat what I want and when."

A sadness latches onto the words, and his voice trails off into nothing. I stay silent, unsure how to respond.

Across the street, I hear someone call his name.

A short guy, twink-like in build, wearing a long jacket over leather pants, runs across the street, face beaming, eyes glinting at the sight of him. When he reaches us, he is breathless and wraps his arms around Nathan and pulls him in for a hug. "It's so good to see you, Nate. Where have you been?"

I step away from them, but the way he held Nathan, pulled him near and now has his hand on his arm is driving me wild. I have taken this guy for my own, which should mean no one else can touch him. I can feel the irrational thought but can't tamp down the fury that comes with it. I'm gritting my teeth, kicking the toe of my lace-up into the cracks in the sidewalk, when Nathan joins me again.

He says: "Sorry about that. He's a friend from work. We wait some of the fancy parties together."

I nod but don't respond, and he can see the way my jaw is set, how my gaze has switched to thunderous, and he doesn't push on.

We walk back to where I parked the car in silence, and there is no more conversation between us, the radio the only thing providing any noise to stifle the silence.

I open the window a crack and try to breathe through the fury, and now we are alone, I calm down. I realize I've lost all the good will the day has built between us, and heading into the evening, I need to regain some of it. Fuck.

We arrive home, and I hold the door open for him to usher him in ahead of me to offer him a drink. A few bottles of wine are still standing on the rack, and I pick the most expensive one and open it, pouring us both a glass.

And he says: "I have to use the restroom."

I point to where it is, down the hall, away from the open space area, towards my bedroom, and he disappears from sight.

Watching him walk away, I know I need to make this better, to regain the lost ground. I shrug out of my jacket, take the wine glasses to the couch and sit and wait for him to return.

It's a long wait, and I finish a glass and refill by the time he comes back to join me. With a smile, he sits and sips his wine glass.

I break the stalemate and say: "So, how was being a tourist in New York? You have fun?"

And he smiles slightly and says: "Yeah, it was really nice." And he puts one hand on my knee and says: "Thank you. I really needed that."

And as if we are old friends, old lovers, I squeeze my hand over his. It's warm and soft, and I want to pick it up and draw it to my face, to run his fingertips across the line of my jaw, to take his fingers in my mouth and suck the way he sucked the tear from my thumb the night before.

He removes his hand, and I feel that desperation wane.

And I can't help myself when I ask: "So that guy? Just a friend from work, or was there a history?"

He furrows his brow and says: "No history. Honestly, just a friend."

I can feel my face turn warm, the blush making a sensory ascension from my neck all the way up to my cheeks.

And he laughs a little and says: "Why? Jealous?"

And I don't know how to respond.

And he says: "I can get you his number if that's what you're asking?"

He says it sincerely—it's heartbreaking.

So, I say: "He's not my type," and I punch the first word for emphasis so he knows what I'm inferring.

He bites his lip and takes another sip of wine, and when he rests the glass back on his knee, I take it from his hand, rest it on a coaster on the coffee table next to mine, and I gently put my hand to the back of his head.

And I say it again. "*He's* not my type." Now he knows what I'm saying. Now I realize the gravity of it.

I'm looking deeply into his eyes, and our faces are inching closer together. I lick my lips and let my gaze fall to his red blossoming lips, full and thick on that slender face.

And with the hand in his hair, I guide his face to mine, and I take what I want from him and kiss him deeply and with the most passion I can muster.

CHAPTER SEVEN

I CAN'T RECALL THE LAST time I had sex. It was back before the date nights took a deadly turn, so it's got to be four years or more. The antidepressants, the isolation, it all just made it something that bore no interest, and I had to find an alternative to make life worth my while, and somewhere inside me, I'd always been that guy. Even when I was young, I was fascinated with blood, with death. I would find dead animals by the roadside and hollow them out, carve them into pieces and see how they'd work. As I got older, it got easier to deny.

Then one night, I just snapped.

And there's something liberating about beating a guy to death with a bottle of craft vodka that just opens a block you've been feeling for years, that sets a part of you you've kept damped down free. That very vodka bottle sits in the back of my closet now, traces of brain and skull still stuck to its thick base, enclosed in a vacuum-packed baggie to keep it fresh.

I think of this for some reason as Nathan takes my hand and leads me down the hallway and into my bedroom. His brazen look from the night before has returned to his face, his eyes lidded in anticipation, his ass swaying seductively as he walks the short way to my room as if he knows where he's going. At this point, I suppose it's the last unexplored area of the apartment, so the process of elimination made the guesswork easy.

When we get inside the door, I close it behind us, and our motion trips the sensor to trigger the bedside lamps. The room is lit in a dull yellow, mood lighting low enough not to jar us from what's about to happen. Nathan turns to me, looks me dead in the eye, and then leans in to kiss me.

My head swims. I'm feeling things I have lost any sense of feeling, the swell of his velvet lips against mine, the slick sliver of his tongue as it probes my mouth. He groans low into the kiss, and I pull him close and devour him.

He unbuttons my shirt, runs his hand down my chest, and rakes bitten fingernails over my skin until the tracks of his path blossom red. I look down at the scratches and then into his eyes again, and this primality there has consumed him. It's the darkest part of him emerging, the part that runs on instinct alone, the part that could kill.

The shirt is discarded to the floor, and his sweater and t-shirt follow, and I can get my hands on the hair that covers his torso, soft beneath my fingers, his skin, this breathing mass covering unadulterated desire. We kiss again, more feverish, hard enough to bruise my lips, and he struggles out of the borrowed joggers and the loaned boxers, his hardness springing free as he returns his arms to my shoulders and lets his fingers caress down my back.

I take my cue from him, unbutton my slacks and let them slide down my legs, pull from the kiss and slide down my briefs, kick them both off clumsily and with all my strength, the wetness of my excitement pressing into his thigh, I pick him up and throw him down on the bed, his body making a perfect indent in the pristine comforter beneath him.

And I'm kissing down his body, letting my tongue explore the ridges between lithe muscles and prominent ribs, tasting bitter copper on my tongue from the dried blood that still lingering on his skin. The taste is intoxicating, and I moan as I lap at it, and he writhes beneath me, his breath hitched to a pant.

He balls his fists into the sheets as I take him in my mouth, swallow the length of him down until his glans passes my tonsils and, further still, buries my nose in the sour scent of his groin. He bucks as I swallow him down, and I release him and take him down again and again, hearing him mewl with every consuming gulp of his cock down my throat. I can taste the sweet flavor of his precum in my mouth, and I hold my cock, rock hard, in my hand and pump.

Then his fingers are wrapped in my hair, in fists, pulling painfully and dragging me closer with every consumption of his length. I pull him from my mouth, spit onto my fingers and wet his hole as I resume sucking, pressing, pushing, and pushing until two fingers are buried inside him, warm and deep.

He's consumed, moaning and panting, his back arching in pleasure, that I have to stop what I'm doing before the whole thing ends prematurely. I remove my hand, let him fall from my lips and climb back up his body, pressing the length of my own prone against him and kissing him once more. He can taste himself in my mouth, his tongue darting out for laps of his sweet flavor as it clings to my lips and tongue. He spreads his legs, and I settle between them, my engorged cock pressed against his.

I can feel his need to be touched, to be wanted, his own loneliness mirroring a feeling inside of me I had long forgotten. The feeling of connectedness only serves to drive the desire on, to make me want him more, to make me need to push myself inside him and fuck him into the sheets.

And he sits up, resting on the bandaged arms outstretched at his sides, his legs spread wide around me, and he says: "I want you to hit me."

And I sit back on my knees and, without thinking, without even questioning why, I raise my hand and strike him across the jaw, hard, my hand leaving a red, palm-shaped print in the perfection of his pale skin. His head snaps to the side in surprise, and he turns from me, and I worry this is over. I'm not ready for this to be over.

And he looks back at me and smiles, takes my hand in his and balls it into a fist, and he demands of me: "Don't be a pussy."

I could kill him if I hit him hard enough, but I not done connecting with him, with his body, binding our souls together through this intimate act which will make the eventual betrayal all the sweeter.

I reel back my arm, and my knuckles connect with a wet thud, his lip splitting at the side, blood pooling and spilling down his chin, my hand protesting with the pain that seems to have invigorated him. He pulls me down on him again, and I kiss the blood from his lip, smearing it onto his face with frantic abandon. I want to drink him down, every ounce of his blood through the gash in his lip created by passionate violence. I want to rip him open and climb inside him.

Instead, I hitch his legs over my arms, raise his ass toward me and plunge deep inside him, not stopping when I meet resistance, not slowing when he cries out. And I plunge inside him over and over again, I let his legs fall over mine, and I push myself deep into his guts, his eyes rolling back in his head, his hands balled in the sheets so tight, with moans of pleasure and pain mingling into a symphony.

I grab him by the bandaged wrists, push them overhead, and hold him down, and he winces as one set of his stitches burst beneath the fabric, as fresh blood starts to pool on the white cotton.

I stop for a second to appraise it, and he says: "Don't stop—it's fine. Keep going."

And like some lovelorn lap dog, I do as he bids. I push myself into him, so our bodies connect with wet thuds. I don't hold back. I don't pull anything from each violent slam inside of him. But after a while, I need to slow down. I'm not done, not nearly. I lean down and lap at the bloody lip, bite it between my teeth so fresh blood drains into my mouth, and I greedily swallow it.

Beneath me, he turns over, climbs onto his knees and presents his fucked hole to me for more abuse. Looking back over his shoulder, he meets my eye and says: "Don't hold back. I can take it."

So, I don't.

I fuck him so hard I think I might kill him; grind myself so deep inside him his moans turn to guttural grunts of astonished surprise. I repeatedly fill him with every inch of me, and he takes every second of the action, every pounding motion swallowed by his accommodation. I spank the pale ass and leave my fingerprints buried in his skin. At that moment, I brand him, I make him mine.

I'm getting close when he pulls away, grabs me by the shoulders, and pushes me down onto the bed, so I'm flat on my back, my dick throbbing and hard, standing upright from my body. And he lowers his ruined hole onto me and fucks himself as hard as he can manage with my cock. He bounces heavily, clumsily, swallowing me inside him, and I can feel myself getting ready to cum.

And then, he reaches down, pulls my hands to his throat, and holds them there, and I sink my thumbs into the dent beneath his Adam's apple and push so no air can pass. With his hands, he massages his dick, faster and faster, still fucking himself, hunched on top of me, his face turning blue. And when he cums, his hole tightens around me, and I have three good pumps left in me before I spill inside him, and his spunk sprays across my chest and stomach.

I don't want to let go of his neck, but in that second, the last thing I want is to kill him. I only want to see the relief on his face when I let him breathe again.

I rest my hands, and he gasps a sharp intake of breath, and the blueness of his face turns red instead. He collapses on me, my softening cock falling from inside him, my seed following out onto the sheets, and he lays his head down on my chest, his hair a curtain that covers his face.

And he starts to cry, his body rocking with every sob that escapes.

I hold him until his body stills until the tears stop. I lay my hands on his back, pull him close, and shelter him in my arms. I have never felt a connection like this, never felt so wholly owned by another human. I never dreamed there was a way to feel like this.

I am gentle with him. I stroke his bruised skin. I gently kiss the top of his head. It's like trying on a new type of shoe to see how it feels. And it feels magnificent.

This kid is fucked up, this much I know. But could he be the kind of fucked up I need?

I hold him as he falls asleep in my arms. And in that second, I think I fall in love.

TAKE TWO:

NATHAN MCGUIRE:

THE DEVIL AND THE DEEP BLUE SEA
HAROLD ARLEN

CHAPTER EIGHT

IT'S THE KIND OF HOTEL you can book by the hour, so that says all you need to know. I've booked it for two but don't plan to stay that long. Everything I touch is sticky; this scent of fresh lemon in the air disguises the undertones of rot and deviance. Somewhere in a nearby room, a hooker screams an over-the-top fake orgasm into the air, and this place, with its weird stains and $20 an hour charges, reminds me of home.

I've not got a bag with me, just my usual keys/wallet/watch shit and a pack of disposable razor blades; it's all I need to make a mess of the shittiest hotel room in Manhattan. There's a black and white TV that's as deep as it is wide, like the ones you would watch cartoons on Saturday mornings as a kid, which I flick on with an audible *pop*, scanning channels until I find the news. The sound makes it feel less lonely, but I'm not watching for the company. The story is all over the news; butchered queer socialite found slain in his loft; witness says the assailant was tall, well dressed, otherwise unremarkable; that's my guy.

Somehow Mallory can walk in and out of places, leaving nothing but a corpse in his wake, and no one can find him except me.

I leave the TV blaring its loop of coverage and head to the bathroom, flick on the light over the sink and watch a roach crawl from the plughole. It's that kind of place. The light flickers twice and then hums this long, drawn-out buzz like a swarm of bees just entered the room. My feet stick to the floor. It's perfect.

I spoke to Wayne, my dealer. He has these huge deep gashes in his wrists from when he tried to off himself. He told me the first cut will always be deeper, and if the case is the same for everyone, the second wrist will barely take a wound. You'll go in with a deep slash right off and sever something important in the wrist and not be able to hold the blade properly with that hand. His left wrist is a mess. His right looks like he punched a window. The difference is in the details.

I splay the razors out on the side of the bath, double-sided and two inches long, the kind you slip into those old barbers' razors for the closest cuts. Everything is ready but me.

In the bedroom, where the TV switches to the weather forecast, frost warnings, and tales of colder times where the city's homeless will freeze if they don't find shelter, a window looks out onto the street. I see the hospital's old red bricks holding up the lofty building. I'm only on the second floor, so I'm close enough to get there before I do any damage that might cost too much.

Hell, at this point, I don't even care if the cuts run too deep; perhaps it would be a blessing.

Wayne told me if I'm going to fake it like this, try to cut the wounds with the blade on its side, fish it up and under the skin, and cut away from the vessels; you'll bleed like crazy, but the damage won't be permanent. It will make for a great show.

I've planned the route, on foot, across the street, and through the doors. And since it's NYC, no one would stop me, bleeding or not, as I walk out of the hotel and across the walkway. It's midday and it doesn't look overcrowded, so it's time to do this.

I don't sit on the sticky bathroom floor in case I make a mess of this and need to get over there quicker. If I sit down, I run the risk of not getting up again, and though the option might seem appealing, I've got shit I need to get done.

Mallory's business card is in my wallet, but I've memorized the details. I'm set.

I fish out a stash of coke from the last of my stash on a key and snort it, doing another bump for courage. It hits everything it needs to, and I'm about ready to start. I look at myself in the mirror, watching from my periphery as the roach disappears back down the drain. "Well, kid, it's time to die," I say to my reflection.

I need to make the left wrist look worse. I hold my right thumb against it and find the pulse. Got to cut around where you can feel the blood flow or risk a quick bleed out. I grab a razor in between my hands and notice the absence of any shaking; I'm not afraid. It's all just part of the game.

With the razor lying practically on its side, I stab it under the skin of my left wrist and make some hatchet sawing motion to part the skin there. I chicken on the first slice, it barely bleeds, like an overgrown paper cut, so I take a breath and hack a bit deeper, and blood starts pissing out of the wound.

I'm quick to make a half-assed attempt at the other wrist, and then I grab one of the shitty yellowing towels hanging by the sink and hold it between my wrists.

It didn't hurt like I thought it would. It felt like I was meant to do it.

Says a lot about me.

The towel becomes sodden with blood, and despite my efforts to avoid the veins, I've got one cut by the volume coming out of me. My left arm is starting to feel cold, and I'm starting to feel a little woozy.

There's blood on the sticky floor but not on my shoes, and I try to avoid stepping in it as I leave the bathroom. I paid cash under a fake name. It doesn't matter anyway.

Soon, I'm out the door, bleeding wrists holding a sopping wet blood-filled towel between them.

I'm down the first flight of stairs, the second, and onto the street. People are milling up and down outside, but no one casts a look my way as I drag my feet and walk the crosswalk to the entrance of the hospital.

And for some reason, I'm crying; I'm unsure if I genuinely feel it, or if it's just a show. But when I get through the doors, a nurse looks at me with wide eyes, and I collapse at her feet, hot blood pouring from the open wounds, hot tears running from my eyes.

Quite the sight, I'm sure.

THEY'VE GIVEN ME LOCAL ANESTHETIC in my arms to sew up the gashes in my wrists and a beta blocker to try and reduce my blood pressure while I regain some of the blood they have had to transfuse back into me. And while a doctor throws these baseball stitches around the inside of my veins, they ask me all the questions needed to fill out the form.

I tell them my name, address in Hoboken, and social security number. They ask me for an emergency contact, and I lay out who they need to call to set the bait. I'm not some old socialite or aging club kid, but I'm betting that Mallory won't resist the fractured, vulnerable kid with the slit wrists to take home as a plaything. I asked the nurse not to mention my name or what I did when they called. I plead with her, my tear-filled doe eyes flashing my innocent request so it doesn't seem odd. I say I don't want to worry him, and I don't want him getting in an accident speeding down here. I lay it on real thick, and the kind nurse behind her mask gives me a sympathetic smile and relents.

This is playing with fire, I know. But this is how it has to be.

When they give me something for the pain, I wipe out and fall into a deep, dreamless sleep, and I can relax a bit.

But when I start to come around, that oblivious narcotic sedation wearing off, he's sitting in the chair by my bedside, making himself at home, going through all my shit in the little plastic baggy they stuffed all my belongings in.

Just like I knew he would.

He's seen the business card.

I'm like a lamb to the slaughter in his eyes.

I watch him lick his lips, and he's taller than I remember,

dressed in these grey work slacks that cover his long muscular legs that seem to go on for days. His hair is a disheveled auburn crop on top of a handsome face, clean-shaven, with a jawline that could cut glass. I don't remember him being this attractive. I don't remember him looking this… normal?

My wrists have started to sting again, and I watch him while pretending to drift off. Until he turns to me. His eyes are striking. There's life there, humanity, which I didn't expect. There's a softness to his expression I hadn't pictured when I'd thought what this moment would be like.

I'm not afraid of him. Every human trait he's displaying gives me the confidence to think I might be able to pull this off.

He stands and helps me sit up, his large hands supporting my back, one holding my arm above where the bandages have sealed my wounds shut. He is gentle. I realize this is all a show to him, something kind to throw me off the scent, to let the nurses release me into his vicious care. A monster knows how to act to lure in the unsuspecting victim, and to him, I'm just some idiot to be reeled in.

But I can be a monster too. When it really counts, I've got a lot hiding inside of me.

I stay mute, let him do the work, let my body emanate vulnerability and helplessness.

Before the hour is through, we are on the Brooklyn bridge and moving towards his apartment, away from the city, and into the lion's den.

CHAPTER NINE

HIS APARTMENT ISN'T BIG AND ostentatious like I thought it would be. It's just a typical apartment, albeit a little sparse. His kitchen looks exactly like this hotel kitchen I worked in as a pot wash on Staten Island when I was thirteen, back when life was simple, back before mom died. Everything here looks easy to clean, and it pounds home the point that this guy is all about the easy cleanup, a bit of bleach, and the crimes just wash away.

I wonder if I'm the first victim to walk through that door or if this is a common occurrence.

Mallory pulls out this expensive wine and pours a glass for us both. I don't typically drink wine, but according to Mallory, it's the preferred drink in his house.

He's charming in a way I can't quite fathom. He's feeding me wine and talking to me like I'm a guest.

When will the other shoe drop? I wonder when he'll strike me down.

But he doesn't. He watches TV with me and keeps

the wine flowing. It's light and easy and I'm very very aware…. He's flirting with me.

So, I flirt back. I figure it's all that's keeping me alive right now. The flirting just feels natural, like I'm being my authentic self, if that self ever had a chance to flourish in this world.

Gradually, I get drunker and more comfortable, and as the conversation starts to flow as easy as the expensive wine, he fetches me a set of clothes to change into. I'm touched, but I can see the way he is looking at me, so I take my chance to buy myself the time and trust I need to get this done.

I strip slowly before him like it's the most natural thing in the world, all the way down to bare skin until I'm wearing nothing but the bandages on my slit wrists. He watches hungrily, lets his gaze take in every inch of skin on display from the top of my head, down my chest, to my soft cock and beyond. I put myself into his borrowed clothes and return to my spot on the couch. Its calculated, all of it, designed to bring down his defenses so when the time is right, I can get everything that I need from him and do the thing I've been dreaming of for six months.

I've never killed a man before, but I've been plotting this for the past half a year and I'm ready for whatever shape or form it takes. I'm not planning on coming back from it, so I don't care how it ruins me. I think perhaps, I've already been ruined beyond repair.

I ask him to chuck the old clothes but keep the hoody. It seemed fitting I wear it tonight, so I chucked it on. It's like I have a piece of my old life with me.

Mallory starts to talk to me as if he's trying to impress me, talking about celebrities he's met in places I don't know and so I ask him questions about himself. I want to know exactly who he thinks he is. I ask him about his life and his job, and I watch him respond like anyone else would.

Omitting the biggest fact of all.

That he is a serial killer.

When he asks me if I have family, I tell him my parents are dead; for some unknown reason, saying that out loud in that room makes me cry.

For whatever part of his twisted game he's playing, he comforts me, wipes a tear from my eye and the proximity is jarring.

Only the hospital knows I'm here. I'm not safe, but his hands on me feel calming.

His body is strong and lean and muscular, and I start to think the worst thing I could think That I could fuck him and not feel a thing That by doing so, I'd at least be splashing this place in my DNA in case they ever need to try and figure out what happened to me.

So, I suck the tear from his thumb, and it's like I've committed some heinous crime. He pulls away from me, gets up and stalks his way to the kitchen.

So, before I can even get his guard down, let alone his slacks, he's putting the wall back up again, like he's got a heart, like he cares at all. The guy is a monster and he's acting like he gives a shit about my feelings. I'll admit, the rejection stings, but I won't push this further than it needs to go. I have all the time in the world to make this happen if I can just keep myself alive long enough.

He just sets this fancy security alarm, tells me he wants to keep an eye on me, and goes to his room. I think thanking him might earn me points, but he retreats like the stakes are so low he can't even be bothered to play the game.

I'm left alone in this strange place, with the TV blaring, knowing I won't be able to sleep. I flick the TV to something vaguely watchable and settle in, and I don't sleep a wink, am too afraid to make a noise by turning the place over, looking for what I'm trying to find, looking for the evidence I need so I can make this all end for good.

When the strip of light beneath his door goes dark, I get myself water from the fridge to rehydrate, to try to figure out how to get through the rest of the night without falling asleep.

I watch a movie, some schlocky horror with machetes and blood that's too red to be real. I know this because when I cut my wrists this afternoon, the blood that did flow was nearly black. It could have been a trick of the light, that orange bathroom with no windows making everything seem darker. Hell, it could have been the cocaine, but when I slashed open the skin, it was like something infected and poisonous came dripping out of my veins.

When the movie ends, I find some late-night talk show to take its place, some dramatic family drama with some balding guy getting everyone to confess these seedy secrets under threat of a lie detector test. I think about what it would look like to drag Mallory onto something like this, to have him admit to who he was, to what he'd done. In the end, the daydream is better than the cringeworthy reality.

My eyes start to feel heavy the more I watch, but I'm

rested enough from the hospital that I know I can skip sleep altogether. I'm not sure I could sleep even if I tried.

At around 4 am I get up to use the bathroom, take a shit, and start to clean up. I want to shower the day off me, want to wash the crusty blood from my arms and my torso, but there's no way I can do that and not wake him up, and no way I can do it without wrecking the bandages around my wrists and causing the sutures to start to pull, the wounds to get tacky and start to stick.

I use a bar of soap by the sink and wash the places I can get to, my face, my pits, my junk, and ass, and use a roll-on deodorant from this little wheeled display stand. He has a collection of men's toiletries, aftershaves, balms, lotions, moisturizers, and under-eye creams. I use a bit of moisturizer on my face and spritz a few pumps of the aftershave into the air. It smells like him, warm, rich, and attractive. It smells like money, like confidence and his whole devil-may-care attitude. I think about splashing some on myself, like I can take on his characteristics by sheer force of osmosis. But that's not how this works. I've been trying to harden up my whole life. It's tougher than it looks.

I hear him get up at around 7 am and use the bathroom. I make my way to meet him on his way out, to prove I'd stayed, hoping it'll mean something, hoping if nothing else it might grant the slightest mercy if this all goes sideways.

As he exits the bathroom, I try to resurrect the vibes I was giving the night before, when I tried to lure him in, when I sucked on his finger. He stands back and lets me in, and I think I make him nervous.

It's not ideal, but it's not nothing.

CHAPTER TEN

Mallory takes me on this convoluted drive around the city. I told him I was a theatre major, which wasn't true; I know nothing about these glitzy Broadway shows he's yammering on about. So, he's showing me some hotel where there used to be a place where a guy worked who went on to write a story about not being able to pay for your apartment or something. I'm bored, but I just nod along.

After hours of making these zigzags across the city, we wind up in Times Square, and I'm acutely aware we are near his offices. I've been staking them out for months, never quite catching when he goes in and out, his attendance not predictable the way it was before the pandemic before working from home became the new normal.

He takes me to a diner, and I order everything I can feasibly consume, building my strength. I don't know how long he'll keep me once the day is over, but for some reason, I'm comforted by the fact he's taken me out in public. Perhaps this is a challenge for him, testing what he can get away with? Either way, I'm forking eggs, bacon, and toast down my throat like a lifeline keeping me tethered to the earth.

I'm still not full when the plate is clear, but it's enough to keep me going. Between the food and the coffee, I feel like I could at least last the next few hours at full strength, but I've found being this hopeless, being this angry, takes energy, and I need to refuel more often. It's easy to ignore when there's coke or pills, but with the last of my stash abandoned in the hotel room yesterday, I'm all out of options for synthetic strength.

Just like he said he would, he drops his jacket and my hoody into some dry cleaners that looks like a front for mob activity. I wait outside, not bothering to put on a mask, not wanting to do anything but breathe deep the fresh air to clear my head.

He leads me away from this dingy laundry to some other tourist trap and I can see he's pretty satisfied with himself. Before long, after paying our entry and making our way up an elevator to the 100th floor of some glass pillar, he leads me out onto this platform that overlooks the entire city.

The view is incredible. From up here, you can imagine that the tiny infrastructure of the city below hasn't been swallowed by rot and corruption, isn't teeming with pestilence, with hatred and crooked forces designed to keep everyone down while they fill their pockets.

From up here, it looks like a nice place to live. Almost.

Then I look right down, over the glass plate panels keeping me from falling to my death. I mean, I really look down. Below, in the plaza outside this fucking massive building, there's this void.

Am I suicidal? Cutting my wrists was my ticket to Mallory. But now I wonder … I imagine how much of my body would be left if I jumped from this platform and let myself fall countless floors until I kiss the asphalt below. It's sick, but I smile at the thought of this all ending.

When he tells me, "It's good to see you happy," or some platitude from some Hallmark movie, I'm reminded why I can't just end it all. I have unfinished business and it's standing at my side, smiling like it wouldn't kill me as soon as it tires of my presence. The smile stops; I don't think there's anything that could bring it back.

He buys me a pretzel from a street vendor with some shitty cart, and when he comments about the way I'm forcing it down, I feed him some sympathy yarn about not getting fed much as a kid. I was never much of an eater anyway, being wiry with no appetite. It was all for the best as we never had the money for these fancy morning breakfasts in tourist-filled diners in the center of the city, or every wild salted pretzel from any street cart we walked past.

Then, from nowhere, like a bad dream, Keenan Wexler is running across the street in these skin-tight pleather pants and some bargain basement faux fur that hangs below his knees. He whips me up in this caring embrace that is wildly disproportionate to the level of acquaintance he is. From my periphery, I see Mallory stalk away.

With my sleeves pulled down tight over my hands, hiding

the bandages that cover my fake suicide attempt, he's asking me all these questions, like where I've been, like what's new, and who's the sexy daddy escorting me round town.

So, I lie, like I always do. I tell him Mallory is a guy who needed a tour on Craigslist and is visiting from out of town. I tell him I needed the extra cash as the events still hadn't bounced back.

That's where I met Keenan, and he too was hit by the loss of catered events. His answer was to cling onto the online sex trade and make himself the cash he needed to survive in low quality online porn. The last time I saw him, he'd tried to recruit me into one of his videos, said he needed a top to make love to him, that his viewers wanted to see him taken care of tenderly, put first and treated with respect. I'm not a top, never have been, and never plan to be, so I used that as the excuse to turn it down.

Truth was, I have one goal and it's to get this finished. I don't need a legacy to follow that. It's one and done for me. Then I'm out.

I wish Keenan well as I watch Mallory kicking holes in the curb with these expensive leather loafers and move back towards him. And he won't meet my eye, he's turned frosty, and I can't work out why.

Perhaps, in a city of millions, he was alarmed to see someone I knew, someone who might be able to identify him to the police if they ever find my body. And they always find the body. If only they had the capabilities to find the killer.

We walk back to his car in silence and listen to the radio on the way back to his apartment, and as we reach his door, it's like he's shifted from one personality to another. He's opening doors like a gentleman, ushering me in, and offering me wine. He's trying to undo the bad vibes of the past hour.

It's dark outside already and I know I need to get this moving. I figure if I can get him to let go, to get him down and rested, then I can start my part of this charade headed where it needs to go. It also crosses my mind that the more of me they find here, the more it'll point to Mallory as the guy who killed me.

Unless I succeed and get him first. It's a possibility, one I appreciate but won't take for granted.

We sit down and it's just unbearable to try and watch him express this idiotic jealousy he seems to have towards a hug from an old friend. He suggests that Keenan and I were more than friends. I shut him down, offer the kids number to him, because I could see a world where Keenan and Mallory are together, both soullessly making their wares from their favorite hobbies, everything on the outside this plastic façade, everything inside just a choking void.

But I flirt to assuage him, and soon, his hand is in my hair, and he's pulling me close. He's implying that I'm just what he likes, and for some reason, some fucked up, beyond me reason, I let myself lean into the compliment. It's been years since I felt seen, or desired as anything more than just a warm body, and I feel like, with the way he's looking at me, the way he has chosen me, that this would just mean more. Even if I do end up just another body in his long list of bodies piling up throughout the city.

When he kisses me, the kiss is so passionate that I decide it's time to make the move.

More than anything, I need something to distract myself from the constant confusion being in this guy's proximity is giving me. I stand up and reach out for his hand, lead him to the nearby bedroom, the only room I've not seen up close since I got here.

The connection starts to build, and he kisses me like he owns me, firm and fast, like he wants to consume me. He pulls off my clothes, throws me down and for the first time since I was a kid, this doesn't scare me. I'm in a room with the most dangerous man I can think of, and I'm not afraid; not the way I used to be when things would get fucked up and I'd have to be traded to pay debts with this dealer and that; not the way I was when I had to live with that guy for months to make right on a deal backed out on.

This guy holds me like I matter, and I let myself be held. I've been with monsters before, and this is no different. He takes me in his mouth and brings me to the edge of ecstasy.

I can't take it, it's too normal, I want to see who is really hiding behind this mask.

I don't know where it comes from, but I say: "I want you to hit me," and without any thought he slaps me so hard my teeth knock together and my head spins.

But it's not good enough.

So, I have him punch me and the pain is like going home. I tell him to be rough with me and he holds me down and fucks me so hard I have to stop myself from the impending climax. I've fucked a monster before, but never like this, never with such connection, never with such passion.

I don't think twice when I climb on top, wrap his hands around my throat and let him choke me as I blow my load. I'm full of his evidence. If I died right now, my body would draw a clear map: arrows straight to him.

But I don't die. When he lets me breathe, I'm sated and filled with euphoria, the kind I've never felt being with a guy, filled with his cum that's leaking out my ass, despite trying to keep it in.

Ruined, I fall on his body while he stares at me with wonder in his eyes. I wasn't expecting him, and he sure as shit wasn't expecting me. I let myself be folded in his arms and let him nuzzle into my hair as I cry. Wrapped in the arms of a killer, whose life's clock is down ticking by the second, one I've come here to kill. I have never felt safer.

PART TWO:

The Real World Is Where The Monsters Are

(RICK RIORDAN)

TAKE ONE:

JACOB MALLORY:

THE PATH TO
PARADISE BEGINS
IN HELL
DANTE ALIGHIERI

CHAPTER ELEVEN

It is getting light when I wake up, alone and exhausted, bruised, with knuckles that are burning in pain. The night before rushes back, and the absence of Nathan is like a knife to the gut. I wonder, *did he leave?*

I find clothes, dress and get out of bed, walk to the lounge where the night before we had … what? Bonded? Is that the right word?

Nathan is sitting, naked at the coffee table, trying to stop the torn stitches in his wrist from bleeding. I sit beside him and I'm silent, but I take over trying to mend what we broke last night. What I broke.

He has a black eye, and his cut lip is swollen. Seeing him like this doesn't feel great. It feels like when you accidentally step on a puppy's paw.

For the first time I get a look at the slash on his wrist without the bandage. Blood still pools in the wound, but it's a clean cut, done with a razorblade or something equally as unforgiving. There's a first aid kit beneath the kitchen sink and I put the bandage back on his wrist and guide his hand back over the dressing, have him apply pressure while I go in search of it.

There is blood on my fingertips as I fish out the first aid kit, and I put them to my lips and taste them, and the taste feels personal, like a shared secret.

I'm ashamed because of this weird limbo where last night was the best night of my life. I want to ask him how he feels, if he regrets it, if he is scared of me. I want him to fear me, in some sick way. My sickness is what's causing this confusion I know. I have substituted the thirst to kill with the thirst to consume.

I grab a clean towel and clear as much of the blood away as I can and use peroxide to make sure it's clean. He barely winces when it touches the open wound, and in me, a sense of pride flashes through me. My brave guy.

I use butterfly sutures to hold the wound closed, and dab some ointment on it to stave off infection. And when it is all held nicely in place, I replace the bandage, and he's good as new, and I vow not to damage the stitches again, quietly, to myself.

We haven't said a word, because it feels like to speak would be to cheapen it somehow; like what we have transcends words, like they would never be enough.

He looks me dead in my eyes and then leans in and kisses me gently, and the sick feeling in my stomach evaporates like peroxide on a fresh wound. The kiss is soft, tender, the complete antithesis to what we experienced last night, and I never thought I would, but I enjoy the chasteness, the sensuality of his gentle affection.

He lays his head in my lap, and I sweep the hair from his face, the bluish bruise on his eye, the split lip, the furious imprints of my fingers in his neck, they all sing to me, a sad and mournful song.

And I graze the bruises gently. I say: "You're all banged up," and he nods in my lap. And I apologize, say: "I'm sorry," so quietly you can barely hear it.

And he says: "I was asking for it."

The phrasing strikes me. Not *I asked for it*, which would be true. But *I was asking for it?*

He looks peaceful laying there. At some point he falls back to sleep, and I lift his head from my lap and lay it on a pillow and step away.

In the bathroom, I take a piss and start to run a bath for him, figuring he can't get his wrists wet, so a shower is out the question.

I change the blood and cum-covered sheets on the bed, put them into a laundry bag to take to my Russian friends in the city. The room smells of violence with a hint of post-coital expulsion. I could get used to this.

I think of my hands on his neck, and I find myself getting hard again. I had him so close to death that I could have ended him then and there, and he would have died willing, lost in the ecstasy of his orgasm. And my blood lust starts to swirl inside me, a need to kill I must fight in order to keep the wrong people from getting hurt.

Is he now the wrong people? Is he my people? One night has caused all the confusion I could ever cope with, but I know I don't want to hurt him anymore, not unless he asks.

And I think, *I was asking for it too*, because I was. I invited him here. I planned to build him up and tear him down. Is he not just giving me the opportunity to do that, and trusting that I don't? I straighten the sheets out and go back to turn off the water running a gentle torrent into the tub.

I wake him up, and lead him, half dazed, to the bathroom, help him in and get him settled. As the hot water washes over him, he winces as it hits his ass, and I know I won't be able to do that to him again any time soon.

But the violence of that unbridled fuck was addictive, it sang to my inner beast the same way a kill does. I know I need to let off steam if I'm to keep my hands off his broken body, so I start a plan to visit the city, to find a victim and subvert the violence elsewhere so he doesn't have to meet that version of me up close.

It wouldn't end well. For either of us.

I wash his back as he huddles in the water, use a cloth to clean the dried blood from his arms and hands without wetting the bandages. I wash his hair and lean him back to discard of the shampoo and I let him lie there, healing in the water, gathering himself and his strength. And while he lies there, I take a shower in the cubical across from the tub, where I can watch him, and make sure he is okay.

When I pull him from the water, I leave him alone in the bathroom to get himself together while I fetch him something to wear. I forgo the sweats for something nicer, a flannel shirt, some long pants, more borrowed underwear, and drop it into him.

He stands and looks at himself in the mirror, his nude body bruised and blue, his face swollen and tender, and through that, he gives me a smile.

I dress myself, something more comfortable because I have places to go, people to see. I pull on some running leggings and a tight tee, some sneakers, and a light jacket, and when I'm ready, hair combed and deodorized and moisturized and everything else I do to make myself feel human, I head back out of my room and sit down on the couch. I forego the addition of a lacquer on the tips of my fingers to disguise my fingerprints the way I normally would. This is different. It's a need with a timer attached. I don't have time for the luxury.

I turn on the news and watch the footage of the TriBeCa socialite who was found murdered in his loft. His name was Clancy Dormand, and he did some unimportant job at some mid-level company producing something for no one in particular. They show his photo and all I can see is a huge, cavernous mouth, laughing, gaping where his neck used to be. And that small, spiraling darkness inside me stirs.

When Nathan emerges, he is dressed in the oversized outfit, pant legs dragging beneath his feet, long sleeves covering where his bandages sit. He looks like a kid who dressed in his dad's clothes. I give him a belt, and when he tucks in the shirt and fastens the pants tightly with it, he looks good, refined, mature, the kind of guy a mother would swoon over, if either of us had a mother between us.

He's combed his wet hair back, and I can see his entire face, angelic but damaged, the wounded boy turned hardened man. And he pulls me to him by my jacket, presses himself against me and kisses me deeply. He doesn't wince with pain from his lip, and it doesn't split. The kiss is powerful and passionate and tastes of fresh toothpaste and underneath it, something real and whole and his alone, his essence.

When he pulls away, he has that lusty look in his eyes from the night before, he no longer seems damaged but whole and wanting. But I have places to go, and people to kill, and the darkness inside me seems eager to go.

I say: "I have to go into the city for a while, just some stuff for work." He looks crestfallen, like he might ask to come with me. "How about I grab some food and wine on the way back? Make you dinner?"

His face lightens and he nods and says: "Sounds good."

I fasten my cell inside my jacket but don't take my wallet. I'll use my cell to buy the food and I don't need the extra items to carry.

I kiss him goodbye, and though my body begs me to stay with him, I leave anyway.

By the time I get outside, the sky has already darkened into that early winter blackness that comes too early in the day.

It takes a good hour to get to the city and the whole drive I think of what I plan to do tonight. I'm unarmed, but that's part of the thrill; a found weapon makes the unknown more exciting. You can't plan for that kind of shit, and I feel that tickle of anticipation somewhere between my dick and my asshole, a tingle of borderline erotic chills. It's nothing compared to the way I feel when I taste Nathan, but it's a close second, and I'm doing this for him, I know.

I find somewhere secluded to park once I reach the part of Harlem I know is synonymous with drug activity and down-and-out shady guys, bums and the homeless—people without people, who won't be missed in a hurry. It's feet from Central Park, so it's rife with quiet places to do the deed and places you could dump a body and walk away without detection. I don't like to park my car in Harlem, but it is what it is.

I'm wearing running gear, so I jog from the back road where the car sits idle and follow the signs of life to where I need to go, the thick beat of rap music pouring from the doors of a shaded bar, the casual conversation of people living their lives outside a bodega. And I cross the street and enter the park and the light behind me gets swallowed in darkness.

This is a different kind of hunt, one I'm not familiar with. Usually, I'm able to use my strengths in my favor, but out here in the winter chill, all I'm relying on is adrenaline, brute force, and happy accident. There will be no *drinks at the bar*, no *back to my place*. I can't let them talk themselves into a self-reverential fervor and distract them with inane questions about family or work or whether the death of their grandmother affected their ability to form lasting relationships. It's just me, dumb luck, and the night air.

So, I jog, further from the city sounds at my rear, slowly appraising my surroundings without seeming suspicious. The park is deserted, not a soul around, so I stick to the shaded running path that snakes through the outer rim of the park, shaded by large overhanging trees and overgrowth, a perfect hiding place should I need it, somewhere off the beaten track to drag an unsuspecting victim.

I'm running for maybe ten minutes when I hear a voice up ahead, maybe a hundred feet in the distance and I slow to stroll, hug the shadows and watch. A man in a dark jacket talks mutedly on a cell phone, staring at the ground, consumed with the conversation. There is no one past him within view and no one behind me when I check. It's just the two of us, alone in a silent pocket of the park.

There's a system to this, and it goes something like:

1)   Assess surroundings, plan entrance, and exit strategies.
2)   Decide on weapon of choice and acquire.
3)   Attack, quick and quiet, no flourishes.
4)   Make the death quick, it's not a torture (though often it feels like it should be).

We're in public so the killing blow needs to be the head and neck, to stop the chance of yelling, to stifle the voice he might use to draw attention.

I'm sweating as I let my gaze shift across the terrain. We are alone, and no one is coming to disturb us. On the ground, I select a fallen branch, thick and heavy enough to knock him down but not too heavy to wield. And I wait for the perfect moment to strike.

I look as he continues to talk on the phone, his tone genial though I can't make out the words. I edge closer and closer.

I'm within ten feet of him when he turns his back to me, and with all the stealth I can muster, I raise the branch high and charge, striking him with a heavy thud on the back of his head.

His cell phone spirals away, and he crouches and holds where the branch hit him, and I drag him off the running path and into the darkness and cover of the tree line.

In an instant it's easy to see the mistake I have made. He recovers quickly from the blow and squares up to me and he's a foot taller than I originally assessed, his broad shoulders wider than my own, his arms thick with muscle and tattoos that run all the way to his gold-chain-clad neck. I don't overthink it and charge him, my branch lost in the darkness, just my hands as weapons. I collide violently with his torso, my shoulder taking the brunt of the force, and feel him strike down at me, his massive fist pounding into my trapezius muscle, which violently snaps my head to the side, pushing me down, knocking the breath from me.

But I don't give myself the chance to feel pain, as he draws his fist back to strike again. I grab handfuls of leaves and throw them in his face, momentarily distracting him so I can lay a hard blow across his jaw. The hand where I'd struck Nathan before is bruised and the force sends a lancet of pain up my arm, mingling with the sting of his previous blow.

The punch barely knocks him off kilter, and he grabs me by the throat and punches me square in the eye, and I go down, my vision swimming, little cartoon birdies floating around my head like some old school cartoon.

I'm on my back in the dirt when he falls to his knees on top of me, and hits me again, and again, and again. My nose breaks, my lips split, and I bleed and bleed and start to lose focus.

And as he draws back for what I believe is the last punch I'll see while conscious, I see the glint of silver in the darkness at his back. A sterling silver cheese knife emerges from the dark, it's two-pronged serpents tongue blade biting into the inked flesh of his thick neck.

CHAPTER TWELVE

THE WOUND IN THE BIG guy's neck pisses blood, some of which sprays on my face and into my mouth, and I watch as he falls back into the dirt, his eyes wide in the grand cavernous overgrowth of the trees. And I watch as Nathan strikes down again and again with the stolen cheese knife, making slashes and stabs that permeate through the thick muscle, through the white cotton of his undershirt, that stain his jacket in iridescent gore.

My head steadies, but my heart is leaping in my chest, and Nathan keeps arcing the blade down and down again. The guy is long dead, but he keeps stabbing, lost in the violence.

I say: "Nathan," but he doesn't stop, and my voice is weak and defeated in the darkness. So, I shout to him: "Nathan!" and he stops.

When he looks at me, blood runs rivers down his face, coating the already gory red hoody that I took from him the previous night. His hair is slick with sinew and sludge and his eyes are wide and wild.

Then just like a photo flash, he looks down at the body beneath him, and his shoulders hunch forward and he wretches, threatening to throw whatever is still in his stomach up all over the corpse.

I fight against every aching bone and muscle in my body, wipe the tears from my eyes and the blood from my nose and I go to him.

Slowly, like a spooked animal, I peel my trophy from his hand, unzip the inner pocket in the lining of my jacket and drop the knife in there where it clanks against my cellphone, not bothering to liberate it of the blood and ichor that clings there.

Nathan sits on top of the cooling body, watching the blood trickle from the multitude of small but ragged puncture wounds he's inflicted, and he is as still as the night.

I lay my hands on his shoulders. We don't have time to fuck around here, we need to move, and we need to do it now. I use the red cotton of his sweater to lift him to his feet, and the motion causes a shock of pain to run up my right arm and into my neck. I wince silently, but he notices anyway, and the concern for me snaps him into action.

He says: "We should get you back home," and the way he says home, like its ours, like he's not going to leave me, fills the part of me still able to feel with this intense sense of calm. It helps me formulate an exit, one that only minutes before seemed so unclear.

I peel off my jacket over the screaming protest from my hand and arm and then the shirt beneath it. And I use the shirt to clean the blood from his face and hair as best I can. He is sodden with the dead guy's insides but when I'm done, in the dark, he can pass for normal. I try the same for myself but the blood from my nose won't stop and so I roll the shirt up into my jacket pocket, pull the jacket back on over my shivering body and zip it tight.

And before we move away, I hold his face in my hands, ignoring all the pain, and I look him square in the face and ask: "You good?"

It's not the motivational speech it needed to be, but he's aware and he nods. I take his hand and lead him back the way I came in, along the running path, sticking close to the darkness.

He stops me, turns, and runs back to where we just came from and is lost from sight for a second. Then he is back with me, and we are running, hand in hand, away from the carnage, towards a shared safety.

We unlink our hands as we reach the exit to the park and cross the road away from the bodega. Under streetlight we look a mess, but the orange hue being thrown off hides the origin of the thick clots of darkness clinging to us. And then we are at the car and driving away and we are free. There are no sirens singing into the night, and soon Harlem and the chaos we left there is just an afterthought.

The city parts before us, and the Brooklyn Bridge leads us home. My worlds collide. But how they intersect I'm unsure.

CHAPTER THIRTEEN

THE RUSSIAN LAUNDRY WILL HAVE a field day with all the blood-soaked items I will have to take in for cleaning. All our clothes get put into the laundry bag with the soiled sheets.

There's a lost and haunted look in Nathan's eyes, and when he looks at me, I feel like he's looking at something on the wall behind me, never quite registering, never quite connecting. I help him into the shower and guide him beneath the water, bandages be damned. I'll change them after I've washed the remnants of the guy from the park out of his hair and off his skin.

He's immobile and lets me run the soap bar across him, lets me scrub the viscera from the hair on his head and hands. Where the cheese knife had gored the man, chunks of torn flesh had flicked back at him, sinewy muscles and tendons and traces of flecks of shaven bone, all sitting in little deposits in his hair and on his face, all stuck in place with a paste made of drying blood and the sweat of exertion.

I run the soap over his chest, and just for a second, he breaks the thousand-yard stare to look up at me. Then he stands on his tiptoes and kisses me chastely. I massage a healthy dollop shampoo into his hair.

We stay there too long, clinging to one another, scrubbing our skin even when it is clean and the water has run clear.

And then, he turns off whatever he is feeling, his gaze becomes present, and he is back with me like a voice in his head has taken over control, has become the man in charge of the body that seemed determined to stagnate.

He towels down his own skin, peels the waterlogged bandages from his wrists, and dresses in the clothes I loaned him the night before.

I follow him, watching his movements, trying to figure out how he is processing what happened, if he knows why I was there in the park, if he saw me initiate the attack. He walks with purpose to the kitchen, grabs two small shot tumblers and pours generous amounts of expensive vodka into each of them and hands me one, and we drink in unison without any trace of celebration.

But somewhere inside, I celebrate. He has killed, and he has survived, and he could be like me after all.

He fills his glass again, takes a second shot, and lifts the bottle to ask if I want another. I decline, but he goes ahead and sinks the second shot in one.

And when he's swallowed it down without so much as a wince, I break the silence, and I ask: "You okay?"

And he nods and shrugs and fills the tumbler with another large measure.

And I say: "You followed me," and he swallows down the vodka and places the glass on the counter and then places his hands, palm down against the chrome.

And he says: "Yeah, I did," and that's all.

So, I ask him, I ask: "Why?" and he stops to think, he looks away from me and he thinks.

And when he reaches the point where he has something he can verbalize, he says: "I wanted to know what was so important in the city that you'd leave a stranger alone in your apartment. Particularly a stranger who's meant to be on suicide watch."

And I blush, ashamed of the way he is seeing me, the lens through which he views me as someone who could abandon him when he needed me. I've never been responsible for my own needs and never needed to consider the consequences in terms of another person.

And so, I ask: "Did you think I left you?"

"No," he says. "But I needed to know what was so important you had to take off and leave me on my own here? I waited until you left, and I ordered an Uber and it arrived just after you pulled away. And I followed you." He pauses.

And with my heart in my throat, he asks me another question, one I was dreading. He asks: "Why did you attack that guy?"

I pour out another two shots, one for me and one for him, and I choke it down. It burns on the way down, but I need the buzz. I'm not a big vodka drinker, so it hits me, and I try and frame an answer in a way that will appease the curiosity without giving away the true nature of the darkness inside me, something he might understand, or at least be able to accept.

And I say: "I don't know," because the truth is too big to explain between mouthfuls of top shelf vodka taken at opposing sides of a kitchen island. The truth could hurt him, and I don't want to hurt him. The truth turned him into a killer.

He asks: "Are you in trouble?"

And I say: "No".

And he asks: "Did you know him?"

And I reply: "Never met him before".

And he asks: "What would you have done if I hadn't followed you?"

And I walk us around the island until we are close to one another, and I turn his body towards me, place my hand at the side of his face beneath his wet hair and look into his eyes. And I say: "Well, baby, I'd have been shit out of luck."

It's not enough, I need to tell him something, but he relents enough to drop the subject, to chastely kiss me with our busted lips, and snakes his arms around my waist, pulls me close so we can share the warmth of our bodies.

And he says: "Baby?"

"You don't like it?"

And he smiles. "I like it a little too much." There's a hint of warmth, but he's wrestling it.

He unfolds himself from my embrace and disappears into the lounge, leaning down to the coffee table where he emptied out his pockets when we got back. He brings something to the counter and places it on the shiny surface. And all I see is this Ziploc bag full of smaller bags of white powder.

I ask him: "Where'd you get that?"

"I took it out of his pockets. He was some kind of dealer."

And he opens the Ziploc and lets the contents spill out on the counter.

I ask him: "What is it?"

And he opens one of the smaller bags, sucks on the tip of one finger and plunges it in. He coats the finger with the powder, brings it to his mouth and rubs it on his gums. And he rolls his eyes, like it's good shit. I figure its coke. My usual dates are big on the coke. It's a status thing more than anything, and I never had much of a fondness for it.

"Molly," he says, and I'm blank in response. "MDMA. It's ecstasy."

I've never done it before, but I'm not saying that. I'm older than he is, but I'm not a prude.

And he smiles up at me and says: "Want to try?"

And I think, *fuck it*, and nod, yes.

THE MUSIC IS ON LOW, its bluesy beat throbbing fast and thick, and I can feel it in every part of my body. Nathan is using my platinum AmEx to cut lines, and I can feel my teeth thrum with energy. I run my tongue over them, over the roof of my mouth and chew my lip. A couple times the cut in my lip splits, but it doesn't bleed. My lips are dry, and I lap at them, and the sensation feels electric.

I can't feel the pain in my neck and shoulder, and my hand feels fine. And in the pit of my stomach, I feel the tingle of excitement and I get why people do this. It feels like when I see blood pour from the body of one of my dates, but it lasts longer and with each line it refreshes itself. It feels like holding Nathan, like sleeping beside him, like someone ground down his essence and bottled it for me to consume at will.

Nathan uses a rolled up twenty to snort a fresh line of molly off the reflective countertop, and with one strong huff, it disappears in his nose. He pulls back, snorts again and pinches his nostrils shut, wipes the remnants from the area.

My broken nose doesn't ache anymore.

I watch as Nathan starts to sway to the music, watch the blue splotches on his bare torso make waves that ripple and writhe with the music, and I can't look anywhere else. I could stand here, in this kitchen, feeling the shock rock through my teeth and tongue and watch this beautiful creature move like this, watch him be free and to exist in my presence.

The vodka bottle is nearly empty, but there's scotch and bourbon and wine, and I pull them down from the shelf and place them with the baggies of white powder.

And Nathan takes the bourbon and pours neat warm liquor into our tumblers, and we sip, and he dances and sways. And I pull off my jacket and let it tumble to the floor, my cell and the knife clanking loudly as they land, and I move with him, move to him and we grind together in time with the beat. I let my fingers glide over his skin, and it feels like silk against my hand, the soft tufts of his body hair like fine flashes of cotton candy, and I want to taste him.

I grind our hips together and I can feel him harden against me, feel myself throb and engorge at the friction of his touch.

I tell him: "You feel incredible. I want to keep you like this. I want you to stay just this way with me, forever."

And he smiles, kisses my cheek, and says: "You're so high," and laughs at me, and his laugh sounds like the ring of a bicycle bell. I pull him close, and I smell his skin and his hair, and it smells like home.

He cuts more lines, and we snort them, and we relish in the feel of our naked skin against each other, and I drink the bourbon and my head swims. I feel ethereal, lighter than I ever have before. I feel normal for the first time since I can remember, since I was a child.

And the way he holds me, makes me feel safe and warm and makes me remember what it feels like to love someone enough not to be cruel and unkind and not to hurt people, not to hunt them or kill them, or to keep myself separated from the rest of the world or to be alone, and I love him for this, and though I've only known him for two days, I can feel this intense connection that I've never felt before like we are one person and our souls are connected.

Everything comes to me in frenetic thoughts, but they all feel amazing. I drink more of the bourbon, and I get thirsty and drink more.

I watch as Nathan fishes a small silver box from his pocket and slaps it against his thigh. The top of the box opens and a thick flame dances out, lit in these amazing technicolor yellows and oranges that take my breath away. I don't know where the lighter came from, but my eyes are fixed on its dancing flame.

And I realize what I'm seeing is a trophy. He didn't come here with a lighter. I know everything he had in the contents of the baggy from the hospital, and there was no lighter. No, he took this from a corpse. And inside me, I feel a kinship to him, like he is just like me.

But soon, my chest starts to tighten.

I'm sweating profusely as I dance to the rhythm of the music, and it starts to get hotter. I am roasting inside my skin.

And Nathan watches me as I sway, and the last thing I remember before the world turns black, before the floor comes up to meet me, is the smile on his face as I lose consciousness.

And the smile is loaded with something dark. Something finite.

TAKE TWO:

NATHAN MCGUIRE:

HELL IS SOMETHING
YOU CARRY AROUND
WITH YOU
NEIL GAIMAN

CHAPTER FOURTEEN

I WAKE BEFORE HIM, AND I watch him while he sleeps. In the faded light of early morning, he seems normal. For the first time, I think of him by name, I think, *Jake is sleeping*. After that, he's just 'Jake'. I guess if you name the monster, it loses some power.

I watch him sleep soundly, for longer than I should, his hair ruffled against the pillows, his mouth slightly open, the tiniest bit of drool pooling in one corner, and I know that while he is so calm, so silent and placated, I could kill him now and be done with it. But I've vowed, I can't kill him until I get back what he took from me. So, I leave him, softly snoring in the soiled sheets of the bed we shared, and I walk, nude out of the room.

His apartment is a one bedroom, and asides from the room I've just vacated, there's a bathroom across the hall, a hallway closet where he keeps coats and shoes. After that, the open space lounge and kitchen. There isn't much space to cover, nor does there look like there are many places one could hide things. If it's here, it'll be easy to find. If it's not...

I don't let my mind go there. I'm on borrowed time as it is.

My right wrist is bleeding through the bandages as I open cupboards and drawers around his entertainment center and haul through the storage boxes on a shelf beneath his coffee table.

His kitchen cupboards are sparse save for dishes and glasses and the few fixings of things he might use to make easy meals on the go, pasta, condiments, and bread. I even check the fridge, but there is nothing but some white wines chilling, water bottles and an old onion, some butter, and eggs.

Beneath the kitchen island, I open empty cupboards and drawers and find nothing of any use, no clues as to what I'm looking for.

A creak from the bedroom lets me know he's awake and I sit on the couch, defeated, and start to pick at my bleeding bandages.

Before I have time to unwind the sodden cotton mess, Jake is beside me, tenderly taking my hand, unravelling the binds, and examining the wound. His face is stricken, like he feels enormous guilt for being the one who tore the stitches, and I believe he really does feel guilt. Which means he's not without it. Which means he's not all bad?

I try to stifle sickness as I think that; try not to chastise myself out loud for trying to conceptualize a world where a serial killer could be a good man. But I was good once. Maybe he and I are more alike than I thought. But had I not come here to kill him? Perhaps parsing on the subject of relative goodness is not my place.

He leaves the sofa, encouraging me to hold the

bandage against my wound and comes back a minute later with a first aid box. I hadn't come across this in my search of the kitchen and so I know there are more places to look.

He cleans my slashes, the gnarled blackened mouth I carved into my arm, still maintaining its inner sutures, the ones holding my veins together, the outer stitch slightly ripped. With the gentlest of touches, he mends me with a temporary fix, applies a fresh bandage, and kisses me.

It's the kiss of someone who cares, not fueled by need or passion, but delivered with kindness, and I'm so tired of trying to figure this out, that my eyes grow heavy, and I lay my head in his lap and fall back into a deep sleep, one where I feel seen, safe, and held.

As I sleep, he moves away, and I feel that contact leave with him. It's like grief; a longing to cocoon yourself in a feeling that makes you mend, even just for a second. It's why I do coke, for that temporary high to make the bad things go away. Now, in this apartment with a man I barely know, one responsible for cleaving my heart in half, I've found a new addiction.

Jake returns after a while and picks me up in his arms like a kid, carrying me to the bathroom where he sits me down in piping hot water. It stings as it touches my bruised ass, but in the best kind of way, the kind of ache and pain that lets you know the sex was worth it. Gently he bathes me, washing the last 24 hours off my skin with such tender kindness I feel like whatever is left inside me will explode.

When I am bathed, when the dried blood and sweat and spunk is clear from my skin, from my hair, he leaves me in the water to wash himself and I take my time to gather myself back into the single person I came here as, gather the pieces that are gradually fragmenting around me and put myself back together.

Jake, showering alone in the nearby cubicle, proves to be the glue.

He leaves me to ready myself, gives me clothes that are too big to dress in. The shirt is flannel and about three sizes too large, made for a man with a wider build, made for someone taller. But the fabric holds this fresh woodsy aroma that smells like his skin, and I wonder if he's worn this shirt before me or if this is just how his belongings smell. I inhale the fabric as deeply as possible.

The pants are too long as well and when he sees me, he stifles a laugh. With a belt, he binds in the excess fabric, and I feel like a man again. It was just a belt, but I see it as some overblown metaphor, something about him having the means to hold me together.

I can't remember the last time I felt like this, and it's killing me that it's with him.

CHAPTER FIFTEEN

I've already ordered an Uber by the time he closes the door, and its ETA is less than a minute away. When he's inside the car, I head to the door, ready to bolt down the stairs and into the ride to follow him wherever he's going.

It was that kiss. Half of me won't trust him not to come back, the other half is wondering what terrible thing he's about to embroil himself in.

As an afterthought, I pull open the closest kitchen drawer, grab the first knife that comes to hand and jam it into the pocket of this borrowed jacket. I don't know why I think I need it, but I'd be stupid not to take something with me to protect myself.

Then I'm in the car, we are following him at a safe distance, and the driver doesn't question this at all. Five goddam stars to this man.

We disappear into the depths of the city, skirting backstreets and operating around the one-way system around central park, into parts of the city I've never seen, into Harlem where I've never been.

Keeping himself as far back as possible, the driver stops a way back from where Jake parks and I pay him through the app, give him his stars and he leaves me in the night air, cold and alone in Harlem.

I don't take my eyes off Jake for a second, his strong frame silhouetted under streetlight in the near distance. It's like magnetism, as I follow him as he jogs through the darkness, to the end of the street where he's parked his car and out into the open of the dicey Harlem street, with the bars and shops all alive and lit for the night. He crosses at a crosswalk and heads into the park and then he is gone, swallowed by the darkness of the tree line, beyond where I can safely follow without him spotting me.

I wait a beat and follow him into the darkness; it just feels right that it goes this way.

He jogs beneath the sparse overhead lights ahead of me while I stick to the darkened line created by the shadows of the low hanging trees. I keep him in my sight but make no moves to speed up. I watch him like I imagine he has watched so many in the past. I think how what I am doing is mirroring his actions, as he pauses in his motion and starts to stalk a man ahead of him.

It makes sense, he's out here, in the darkness, stalking the night.

I let myself believe a man could be good, even when carrying out the worst atrocities. But as I watch him stalk a human being, it's hard to grapple with the goodness I foolishly believed in. I'm tempted to leave, to turn and return to Brooklyn, to use the time to turn over his apartment and find what I need and just leave. Let him live his life; let him kill. I don't have to become this if I don't choose to.

I'm about to turn around when he creeps slowly from the trees and strikes the man in the back of the head with a fallen branch.

I can't look away. I hate to admit this, even to myself, but I am rooting for him to make it through this on top.

I can't leave, as I see him haul this huge guy into the shade and privacy of the neighboring trees. When they are out of sight, I run from where I watch, and I listen in the dark and train my ear for the sound of the fight.

Branches and twigs crackle beneath my feet as I move, and to me they sound like gunshots, but it does nothing to distract the two men from the fight. In the darkness, I can make out their shapes, the larger man throwing punch after punch down onto Jake, connecting with loud wet thuds to his face.

Jake doesn't try to resist as the fight drains from him.

Then, before I know why I'm moving, the knife is free from the pocket of my jacket, and I'm shoving it straight into the neck of this guy in the dark. His blood bleeds black from the wound, and the rounded upper blades of this weird ornate knife rips through his flesh like it's just cold meat in a butcher shop. When the guy falls backwards away from Jake, when he lays flat on the ground clutching his neck wound, the open sucking pull of his breath coming ragged through the wrong opening, I plunge the knife into him.

I am thinking of nothing but Jake, that he is mine; mine to kill.

I stab over and over again until he stops moving, but the adrenaline is narcotic, and I can't stop my arms swinging the knife down again and again. Everything in my vision goes black, and I lose time.

But when it returns, I can taste blood in my mouth, and the body beneath me is pissing its contents out of these violent tears made with a knife not meant to stab, but to rip. For a second, something in my head says to stop the bleeding, and I reach down before I look at his cold, dead eyes staring up at me.

I open the front of his jacket to view the wounds in the dim light, and something white falls from his inner pocket.

Then Jake is at my side, taking the knife from me. He takes off his shirt and for the second time he cleans blood from me. His face is a mess, but I can't imagine I look much better, and when he has cleaned enough of the gore off me, he pockets his shirt and leads me away.

In my head, all I can think is, *I'm a killer. I killed a man. I'm just like him.*

I didn't have to save him, but I did. So, I tell myself it was because his life is mine to take.

But in the dark, as he holds my hand and rescues me from this mess, I might just owe him my life in return.

I stop and return to the gored body, lift the white package from his inner pocket and stuff it into mine. Then I rummage in the guy's pants pockets to find something, anything I can use later, and find a zip lighter that is mine to take. I tell myself it is not a trophy, that it's not like that at all. But I know, in Jake's eyes, this will win me points. If nothing else, it might get him to speak up about what he's been collecting from his victims, something to get me closer to why I came.

I feel psychotic even thinking like this in the wake of the bloody execution I just enacted on a stranger in this public park, but I'm on borrowed time here, and every move is necessary.

And the white package might just be key if I can use it right.

He is waiting where I left him, looking around, checking the exits we are about to take. When I look at him under streetlight, the blood from his busted nose, from his ripped lip, it just looks black, like war paint. And in a way I suppose it is.

I am bereft when he lets go of my hand, but I walk quickly beside him, letting him lead me wherever he wants. At this point, I would follow him into hell. Or at the very least, I would let him take me there. It's where I belong.

As we drive away from the city, I can feel the blood cool on my skin again, its thick syrupy consistency congealing in the cool night air. I fight the urge to take his hand in mine.

When I plunged my knife into the guy, something inside me changed. I can feel it now, like I don't fit inside my body anymore, like there's a beast inside I'm trying to contain.

I stare blankly ahead and just listen to the white noise of the engine turn over and over and wonder if my beast will grow, and if it does, will I be able to control it.

And it's all about control, right? Maybe that's why he was out there tonight, hunting some stranger in the dark? Maybe he needed to tame the beast inside?

But if that's the case, did he do this, did he leave and go far away to avoid hurting me?

I try to stop the warmth that comes with that thought

but it's impossible. I've never belonged to someone in such a carnal way. If he chose to leave to let the pressure gauge off the darkness that broils inside, then maybe, just maybe, the safety I feel in his arms could be real.

I know, this can't go on the way it is. I can't go on like this. I can't let him get inside. Because I came here for one thing and one thing only. This ends tonight.

CHAPTER SIXTEEN

AGAIN, HE'S TAKING CARE OF me. He's washing fragments of dried bone, flesh, and skin from my body. He is vast and hulking compared to me and handles me like I might break. All the while, I stay silent and let his strong hands cover me, and I can't help myself when I look up and kiss him. He tastes like safety, and I hate that I feel that. But I do. I could hide in his shadow for the rest of my life, but this road only goes one way.

I can't do this sober. I can't do most things sober. And when partially dressed, I pour cold vodka into brittle glasses. Drink and pour and drink until my head swims. Nothing ever seems impossible when you add alcohol to the mix, though I really crave the sweet oblivion of cocaine, of meth, of something to make this next part easier.

But then I remember. The white powder. And I know exactly where this night is going to go. By morning, it will all be over.

I'M SHIRTLESS, CUTTING LINES OF Molly with his credit card on the chrome countertop. I'm high, but I've been faking half the lines. He's been doing most of the gear.

His eyes have found that euphoric state you get to right before it all goes downhill, and when he pulls out the bourbon, I know he's on his way out.

Though it would be easy, I won't let him die like this. I need him down and out enough to subdue.

We dance groin to groin, and he kisses me again, too much tongue, but there's a wall up now, one in which his smile and taste can't break through.

His eyes start to glaze, and he starts to fall. I smile because it's time.

First, I place a cold compress against his head to try and bring down his body temperature. I run the cloth over his neck and cheeks and check him for breath. He's still breathing. So, when I'm sure he'll stay that way, I put all my energy into hoisting him up, pushing him against the chrome counter, and then more power to lay him back and drag his sweating torso further onto it until he's lying across it prone, his limbs outstretched.

I find the cupboard where he keeps the first aid box, household tools, cable ties, and thick reels of coated tape.

Carefully, I bind him there, spread open wide, at my mercy. The only thing on my mind is to take back what he stole from me.

Even unconscious, Jake looks peaceful, like the darkness never came for him. In a different life, I imagine the man he could have been, strong and stalwart, a safe port of call in a storm.

As I bind his hands, there is still the faintest trace of blood beneath his fingernails. It's a sobering reminder of what he is.

There is still blood beneath *my* nails. My monster matches his; we are torn from the same gore-soaked cloth. A part of me wants to know where his horrors started, though I know there isn't time.

When I'm confident he's contained, wrapped tightly to the surface with the cable ties and the thick electric tape, I open the drawer for a weapon, something threatening, something to rinse the answers out of him by threat of violence, a threat I am now more than aware I am capable of following through with; a meat cleaver meets that call. I hold its dense weight in my hand, and it feels like it belongs there. It's weighted perfectly to destroy.

I inhale, ready to begin.

I bang the heavy blade down on the counter, and he doesn't respond. His chest still rises and falls, he is breathing but just not conscious. I fill a glass of water and throw it over his face, and he twitches.

His eyes start to flutter.

I give him a moment to orient himself before I clear my throat to announce my presence.

"Nathan?" he says, through his dry, parched lips, and even though the sound is little, it strikes something inside of me that I was the one he called for when he woke up.

It's this feeling that leads me to the tap, filling a water glass and gently lifting his head to drink.

"Am I tied up?" he asks me, and I nod silently while he tests the restriction of his binds.

He sips at the cup and looks me dead in the eyes. "What's going on?"

Now, I know it's time to explain. But where I start, I have no idea.

The beginning seems like a good place.

I NEVER HAD A DAD; according to mom it was a one-and-done kind of thing, and being catholic, she couldn't do a thing about me but carry it through. My brother, Danny's dad had left years before, so it was just the three of us, though my brother had taken off into the city shortly after he turned eighteen, leaving me and mom to fend for ourselves.

But my mother, for all her good qualities, struggled mentally, and when I was thirteen, I found her in the lounge, a 9mm gauge bullet had blown the back of her head all over the family portraits we'd taken on the pier when I was little. It wasn't her fault, and I know she tried, but I was a thirteen-year-old kid with few options.

She didn't own the house and had nothing in savings. We lived from one paycheck to the next. Aside from a few family heirlooms that my brother hocked at pawn shops, we had nothing to inherit.

Except my brother of course; he inherited me.

That would turn out to be where the real problem started; non-existent father or severely depressed suicidal mother had nothing on what life with Danny would become.

I moved into the city, into the apartment he was renting with a few friends; to social services it was a better choice than making me a ward of the state, and even the pleading look in my eyes when the social worker left wasn't enough to change their mind.

So, I stayed, and at first, I was safe; at first, I had a roof over my head and meals to eat and I got to school on time. At first, I was just a normal kid; until I became useful. I'd seen hell before, the downward spiral of my mother was no picnic for a kid, but there were more horrors than that in the world, and Danny didn't care enough to spare me from them.

Instead, he fed me to them.

Instinctively, I walk around the table so I can be closer to Jake, so he can see what I'm feeling as I recount what led me to him.

His face is pinched in confusion, anticipation. It warms the heart.

So, I go on.

I choose not to tell him the worst of it, on the one hand it wouldn't matter and on the other, there are certain parts of that time that even I can't recall, repressed somewhere in the back of my head, my mind protecting me from going the way of my mother. I'll get there eventually, no doubt, but not until I've got everything I came for.

At first it was just little things, delivering packages and shady baggies of unknown contents. I could handle it, and because I was small and scrawny and had the innocent look of a kid about me, I could get in and out of places without drawing too much attention.

But by rote of my size, I got called in for more pressing work, my tiny frame able to fit through cracked windows, my skinny arms able to snake through mail slots and jimmy locks from the inside.

But a growth spirt gave me a promotion, and I had little else to give except a warm body.

Eventually all I could provide was something I had no concept of at that age: sex and violence. Danny would use my growing body to feed the curiosity of his more depraved clients. The sex admittedly was infrequent, and I was grateful for that, but more often than not, he would trade me for a hit, or as a guarantee that what he owed wasn't far behind. There was one guy who just liked to kick the shit out of me for hours, relentless punches and kicks until I was bleeding inside and out. I didn't have medical insurance, so a bunch of wounds healed wrong and at one point, I had to learn to walk again.

Jake closes his eyes for a second, and then opens them, and I swear to any God who might exist, forming in the corners are these unshed tears; the ironic tears of a monster for the kid who grew up with monsters.

I got out when I was seventeen. Danny was too far gone, too strung out and too useless to stop me and I'd grown up big, despite everything holding me down.

I didn't see my brother again for years. I thought he must have died, the way he was going. He must have owed the wrong guy money or skimmed a little too much off the top or dived into his own supply.

So, imagine my shock when last year, I'm working downtown at some fancy fucker function, and who should walk in but my big bro, all cleaned up, not working the party, but attending.

In the intervening time since I left him, Danny had managed to clean himself up, he'd got out of that life, went to a court mandated rehab facility upstate, went to night school and got his GED. Hell, he'd even come out as bi. And when Danny saw me, his sincerity was appalling.

I felt angry. Danny was at this benefit for the rainforests or endangered species or climate change, some congratulatory hand job for rich people to make themselves feel better about being awful, glued to the arm of some impossibly hot guy worth millions.

And here I was wearing a little bowtie and sweating, carrying crab cakes.

Danny was waiting when the party was over, and he told me he wanted to reconnect. He never mentioned what he'd done to me. He talked too much about how he'd made good of his life.

I can tell Jake is enthralled with the tale, but I'm not sure when in the recounting I reached down and held his hand. I pull it away as soon as I realize I'm doing it, and for a second, he looks like a lost kid, the way I used to look before life gave me my demons and told me to deal with them.

"I'm sorry for what happened to you," he says, but he doesn't know what he's apologizing for, not really, not yet.

My other hand clenches around the meat cleaver, my palm is sweating and I'm itching to swing.

I tell him, the rich guy didn't work out for Danny. I met with my big brother, curious to see if he'd ever try to make amends for the shit he put me through. But it was always the same, a fancy lunch, perfunctory conversation, *see you later*.

I knew, knew in my heart that I had only one thing I wanted in this world.

"Until one night, when I'm walking to his apartment," I say, and I take a beat to breathe.

Jake is silent, his eyes fixed on mine, and I meet that gaze with all the rage and power I can muster inside myself.

"That's the night I first saw you."

CHAPTER SEVENTEEN

JAKE'S FACE HAS CRACKED LIKE some porcelain drama mask, fractured into confusion and speechlessness, and his skin has a waxy pallor, the result of the impending comedown or the shock revelation.

"The door to his apartment was open when I got there. He was already dead. I couldn't do anything to save him, even if I'd wanted to."

He starts to fight his bonds, the muscles in his bare arms erupting into thick ropes as he pulls against the several binds of wide tape holding them in place by the wrist.

"I have never seen you before the hospital," he says, his voice shaky, unsure.

"I didn't say you saw me, but I saw you," I reply.

He's getting agitated, worked up in his fight against the binds, a fresh sweat erupting on his forehead and in the muscular cleft between his pectorals. "I don't know any Danny McGuire! I never have!" He yells his words. They ricochet around the sterile room.

Then, I smile. "Wilson," I say. "Different dads."

He repeats the name out loud. "Danny Wilson?"

I reply. "Nice apartment, upper west side. You gotta remember the vaulted ceilings, the beams across the roof? Perfect place to leave a guy hanging."

Jake freezes, the hint of recognition breaking way into a tidal wave of memory.

"Daniel Wilson," he whispers.

"Yeah," I say. "My big brother. And you killed him."

All the fight leaves his body. He knows I know, and I've got him to rights. There's no getting out of this now, and the realization spreads through him, each limb and part of his body just relaxing in defeat.

I let the cleaver fall against the metal and drag it across the surface as I walk away from him, towards his feet, to the foot of where he is tied down at my mercy.

"You know," I say. "I wasn't the one to call it in. I locked the door behind me, left, and didn't say anything. I didn't want to be tied to that in any way. It was the downstairs neighbors who eventually made the call."

He closes his eyes again as I look up at him, and I move fast back around the table, grabbing him by the hair until his eyes snap back open. And I say, "The way you strung him up by his feet, slit his wrists and throat, every drop of his blood drained out like cattle in an abattoir. And after a week or so, all that blood...." I pause for effect and release his hair. "It showered blood in the apartment below." And somehow, I laugh. "You sick fuck." The words aren't angry. They just sit there, an observation more than an allegation.

After a moment, he speaks. "You said you hated him.

What does it even matter?"

I slam the cleaver down onto the table, inches from his face. I scream at him, "It should have been me who got to kill him! I'd been planning to kill him since I first saw him again, and you took that away from me. Every thought, every sleepless night spent picturing how I'd take everything from him, and you snatched it away in one night. And for what?"

He doesn't answer.

"For what?" I scream. "A cheap thrill?"

From somewhere deep inside me a dam breaks, and the tears come from somewhere deep inside me, and they won't stop. I sob and sob when I realize it's really over. I can't get my life back or take Danny's away. Everything past his death led me to Jake; now this is over too.

I don't know why, I couldn't ever tell you why I seek this comfort, but I lay my head on his chest, and let my tears fall into the ripples of his muscles, let my body rock and sway with these inhuman sobs.

If he could, his hands would be in my hair, comforting me, which makes it all the harder.

When the tears cease, and I can breathe in the woodsy aroma of his sweat and his skin, my mind sharpens again.

"You collect trophies." It's not a question.

He tries to look innocent as I wipe the tears and snot from my face with the back of my hand.

"I know how you operate. I've been following your work for months. Where are the trophies?"

His eyes narrow, and he doesn't say a word. He knows now that my being here was not dumb luck, not a chance encounter with some helpless victim. He knows that I meant to be here every bit as intentionally as he brought me here.

"Just tell me where they are!" I shout, and I slam the cleaver down again, missing his fingers by millimeters, the small gust of wind it creates making him flinch back away from my wild blade.

"Okay! Okay," he says. "But I tell you where to look, and you let me go right? I give you the trophies, and it's done."

I nod.

He exhales, defeated, and he replies with barely any volume to his voice. "There's a loose board in the coat cupboard in the hallway. Everything I collected is under there."

Motivated, I move without thought, through the lounge, down the hallway to the closet at the end, the sensors on the lights announcing my way.

I rip open the door and fling myself down, throwing shoes and gym bags and umbrellas out of the way.

It's there where he said it would be, a board that doesn't quite lie flat, that wobbles in its unsecured position when you lean on it. One side forges up as I press, and it comes away in my hand, and beneath the loose wood, plastic bags, Ziplocs, and air-sealed plastic coat... a thousand keepsakes. I pull them out in creased handfuls, searching the depths of that dark tomb for the one thing that would make this all worth the effort, for the lost treasure that will spackle the hole inside me left by neglect and rage.

I find it finally.

Jake has managed to kick one foot loose from its binds, but it doesn't matter, I don't care anymore.

I pop the seal inside the tiny bag and shake a trinket into my palm. I say out loud: "it was my mothers," as I lift the tiny faux gold cross up and fasten it around my neck. It was hers and then it became something Danny had stolen from me.

With the theft, he condemned me. And just like that, it's over.

Jake looks at me. "Nathan, I'm sorry."

I walk to him, my mother's crucifix, bought from a catalog, radiating strength around my neck. The meat cleaver rests in my spare hand, and I hold his face, kiss him, and let that single tear of joy run from my eye onto his pale skin.

"It's okay," I respond, though the words are hollow.

I raise the cleaver high above my head and watch him close his eyes, before I slam it down, hard enough that it bites through everything, and buries itself into the chrome countertop.

In the deafening silence of this kitchen, I leave without looking back.

CHAPTER EIGHTEEN

When I get out of there, it's freezing, and I pull the sweater I took from the back of the couch on my way out around me tight. I bury my hands in the sleeves, and it smells like him, like arrogance and confidence, like something I'll miss when it's gone. I think of pulling this into a plastic baggy like Jake would, keeping it as a trophy of my time with him, and preserving what's left of his smell when I get where I'm going.

But where am I going? I walk as far as my legs will carry me, but the adrenaline and the molly are wearing off quickly, and before I reach the end of his street, my knees give out, and I'm on the floor, back to a low wall beneath a street sign, staring out to the lilac sunrise in the distance.

What's left now? Killing him would have done no good to me at that point.

Danny's already dead, and there is no bringing him back. I couldn't have claimed his life for my own because, underneath it all, I am not a killer, despite what I did to that guy in the park.

Here I am, walking away with nowhere to go. Everything I had, everything I'd been geared towards, is over, it's just a cheap piece of golden jewelry hanging around my neck, and that's all it has amounted to. Ahead of me is a shithole apartment in Hoboken and the endless promise of catering waiter jobs until I find something to make it all worthwhile.

Behind me is darkness. Jake may be a monster, but I've proven I can breathe in darkness. It's not nothing.

Jake sprints up the street and is at my side. I didn't kill him because I'm not the monster I thought I was. I just love to play in the darkness.

He looks down at me. Duct tape still hangs from his wrists and one leg, but he doesn't say a word. He sits down beside me, and puts his arm across my shoulders, and in the comedown, the confusion, and the tiredness, I let myself lean against him and honestly cry for everything. Especially the nothingness that lies ahead.

I think of the observatory platform, all those feet above the ground, and how good it felt to imagine diving to the plaza below. The tears don't stop, and Jake kisses my hair and pulls me tight to him, and after a while, I relent. I snake my arms around his waist and pull him closer. I want my tears to soak him, maybe even drown him, but that's a silly idea. He would only drown himself in blood.

I realize he's wearing my hoody. I'm dressed up as the monster, and he as the victim. Maybe we are rubbing off on each other? Can you change a person just by loving them?

This is the closest I have gotten to love since my mother blew herself straight into the afterlife.

When my tears stop, he climbs to his feet using the wall at our backs as ballast and pulls me up after him.

With the most tender of touches, taking my hand in his, his own still wrapped in the bindings I left him in, he leads me back down the street toward the apartment.

I go because I want to—because I can't imagine a life without him—I can barely imagine living through each day despite the promise of it feeling a lot like stepping off a ledge.

CHAPTER NINETEEN

WE LIE AWAKE IN BED as the sun rises, and he never lets me go. And we talk candidly, openly about the way things have to be. There are no more lies or pretenses to hide behind. There is nothing left to gain from holding back. I know he won't kill me, and he knows I don't have it in me to kill him. All that's left is what we are willing to do.

"Could you give it up?" I ask stupidly, knowing what the response will be.

He's silent for a moment, not because he's considering the question, but because he's framing an answer in a way he hopes I'll understand.

When he's ready to speak, he does so in a hushed tone. "I've always been this way," he says. "And I don't think I will ever change. Doing what I do, it's necessary to keep me on track the rest of the time. I don't do it because I'm cruel or to feel big and better than everyone else. I do it because it's all I know how to do to keep the darkness from swallowing me. And I know that's selfish, choosing my own salvation over the lives of others, but I only advocate for myself, because if I don't, no-one else will."

He pauses, and pulls me to him, plants a small kiss in my hair. "I won't stop, but I can promise I'll never hurt you," he tells me.

And I believe him.

We talk about it more, and he admits it's a sickness. I can't judge because I'm sick too. My sickness has infiltrated every part of me, and while his urges him to destroy, mine is pointed internally, and I'm the only person I really want to hurt. We are two sides of the same coin, monsters dancing in the dark.

"If you stay with me," he says, "I'll give you everything you could ever want. I'll give you a life, and all the love you could need. You'll want for nothing. But sometimes, I'll have to go out, and when I come back, you'll know what I've done. You don't need to have any part of it, but you have to decide if you can bear knowing what I'm doing when I leave for the night."

It's honestly the best offer he could make, one that I should jump to, knowing what I know about the lengths he would go to keep me safe and happy. But I imagine him out there alone, like the night before, in the park, with all his cards dealt, giving up and giving in. And I know there's no way I can let him go out there alone.

So, I say, "I'll come with you. You need someone to watch your back."

His chest muscles tighten as he smiles, and I don't need to look up to know the smile is wide and goofy and all the things about him that would have made me love him if either of us had just been born normal.

He hesitates, before he asks me the thing I've been dreading. "Would you ever want to…?"

I know what he's asking, but that isn't my truth, that's not my journey. I can love a killer, I can belong to him, but taking life is where I draw the line for myself.

But I wonder, without saying a thing, if the occasion came up, would the darkness in me ever want to try?

That's when I see it, the marriage made in hell, the perfect match of our darkness that led us to be this way. For whatever reason, it makes me feel better.

I'm not saying I would. But I'm not saying no.

We fall asleep against the early morning sun, and we enjoy each other's bodies until it's dark outside, and when night falls, we play House. It's a fucking haunted house, but it's ours, mine and his, and it is what it is.

PART THREE:

The Scariest Monsters Are The Ones That Lurk Within Our Souls

(EDGAR ALLAN POE)

CHAPTER TWENTY

Six months later.

We are on a "first date" in some squalid basement apartment in Queens, drinking ouzo from a red Solo cup, when Nathan tells me he pricked his ankle on a used hypodermic needle. I think, *thank fuck he's on PrEP*, and mime kissing my hand and putting it against the pinprick of blood there. It doesn't get the smile I wanted. It's no wonder in this shithole. I lick the drop of blood from my hand.

This guy is some forty-something night gremlin. He has a gamer setup and no sofa, and I'm finding it hard to fathom what I can use to kill him that will not kill me in the process. MRSA is no joke, kids.

The whole place smells like cotton candy and Cheeto dust, and there is no built furniture save for some old bookshelves and the desk where his gargantuan television is swallowing half the wall. We had to walk downstairs to get into the place. I wonder if this guy's mother lives above where we currently are, looking desperately to see if I can find a knife or a corkscrew or something that will open a vein enough to give me what I need so I can get us the fuck out of this place without needing a tetanus booster.

Nathan walks over to the ancient sagging bookshelves, pulls a Blu-Ray off the top shelf, and scans the back, and the sterile repetitive dance track this guy put on vibrates through the floor, up into the beanbag chair I'm sitting in, and straight to my taint. I want this over with, I want to take Nathan home where we can be alone, and this isn't moving fast enough. I never usually get this restless, but this guy was a wrong choice from a room full of bad decisions, and I'm hoping that, judging by the way he lives, we can forget about this whole ordeal and move on with our lives.

Either the guy has the worst taste in music, or this is one single track played on a fade-in-fade-out loop because everything sounds the same. He sits in his gaming chair, firing first-person rifles at Nazis, and I ask him: "Have you ever had your guts ripped out through your asshole?"

Nathan looks at me from beside the bookshelf, stops scanning his movie case, and cocks a crooked smile, and my heart warms. That's the first genuine smile he's given me all night. But it's not real. I know a real smile on his face, and that was far from genuine. He doesn't want to be here. I want to be here even less.

The guy says: "Huh?" and I know the preamble is wasted on him.

I fight awkwardly to stand up from the cavernous depth of the old beanbag chair, get on my feet, gulp down the last of the bitter ouzo, and motion to Nathan with a thick HDMI cord on the floor. He's uninterested, and waves his hand, which I know is universal sign for "no thanks, have at it." I never stop trying to get him to participate, but he never relents. It's wasted effort, more a routine. I keep thinking, *I'll make you a killer yet*, but he is made of stronger stuff than bending to my desires. If I was in danger, he'd be there, all trepidation gone, swinging a knife or a claw hammer or brandishing a high E guitar string as a lethal garrote if I needed him. But that's as far as his killer instinct goes. He protects what's his, and he doesn't stand in the way of me doing what I need to do. It's a sacrifice, but it takes its toll.

I sigh, wrap the cord around both my fists in a winding motion, and try to do the best I can to put on a show. For some reason, having Nathan watch me do this is essential to the thrill.

The music crescendos to a predictable climax as I grab this aging hipster from behind, lace the cord around his neck and pull it so tight I feel the blood stop flowing in my fingers. I swivel the chair to face Nathan, so he can get a good view, but he just turns, puts the Blu-Ray back on the shelf, and pulls down another one, bored.

When you cut off someone's air supply like this, even from a vantage point of the rear of their body, their neck muscles swell to this optically satisfying roundness, like a puffer fish when threatened; I guess there's some biological imperative to it like the victim is trying to appear larger, more threatening. Not only does it not help them in any way, but it also makes the strangulation and suffocation quicker. I don't like doing it this way, but all I could find by way of weaponry was an old fork in a molding box of

Chinese chow mein noodles from some low-quality Turkish takeaway. There is no blood, and my hands are starting to sting with the length of time I have to pull on the ends of the cord to make this guy die. He pisses himself while I'm yanking hard enough to turn my fingers white, and his khakis turn this sour brown color in an endless trickle that makes it all the way down one pant leg before it stops.

Nathan takes the disc from the case, inspects it for scratches on the reverse, then nods approvingly before putting it back in the case and the case into his jacket pocket. That's his trophy for the night, though he'll get some use out of it before it goes into plastic and under the floorboards. Watching Nathan as I struggle to murder this guy is like watching some late-night browser in a Blockbuster video; he's so turned off to what's happening he can barely elicit a response.

This old, handle-bar-mustached motherfucker has bitten the tip of his tongue off by the time he has the good grace to die, and I choke him for a second more, for good luck, before unraveling the cord from around my sore hands. The cord is coming with me; too many fingerprints for deniability. And I didn't apply the lacquer I usually would before we left the house, hard pressed for time.

When you strangle someone, they don't die from choking, and it takes longer than you think it would. The thing that kills someone with strangulation is usually asphyxiation, a loss of oxygen. Sometimes the arteries in the neck might tear and cause a stroke. You might trap too much blood in the brain by blocking off the jugular vein. Or pressure in the internal carotid arteries in the neck can cause the heart to beat out of time and cause a heart attack. Judging by the color of this guy's face, I will guess asphyxiation, but I'm no doctor.

Nathan is still pilfering media from the corner collection when I walk over, tired, sweating, and breathless, and ask: "You okay, baby? You barely touched your victim!" and I smile with my tongue out, like a faithful dog because he loves it when I do that.

It barely gets a smile. Nathan kisses me, pockets a small paperback, and moves to the door. Date night is over. He looks back at the blue, bloated dead guy, and then his brow furrows as we make our way home.

The night is silent and summer-still. I take his hand, and we walk all the way back to our apartment.

He ignores me when I ask what he managed to take from the dead guy's collection. He squeezes my hand and remains silent for the walk, the discs in his pocket rattling with every step, loud against the profound silence of the early morning.

When we reach the apartment, we settle together, and he hyper-focuses on the burgeoning bruises around my knuckles where the cord bit tight, more consideration than he gives to anything else. He lifts my hands to his mouth and kisses them as if his lips could mend any ill. I'm not entirely sure he is wrong: He has restored every part of me except the darkness inside, and perhaps that's just too beyond repair to ever be fixed.

He says: "Does it hurt?" His face is folded in a concerned look—the real Nathan—as if he didn't know how I got the bruises.

And I smile and say: "I'll be fine, don't you worry about me, baby," and I kiss him with force and passion to let him know what it means that he cares about me, that I see him, and I love him and that it's all going to be okay. He needs the reassurance as much as I need the body count. It's a tradeoff, but it's hardly fair with the cost to him.

When we climb into bed, we make love. He doesn't beg me or guide my hands around his neck. Rather, he looks me in the eyes. The feeling of holding him close, of tenderly being inside him, makes me want to cry. I am the luckiest guy in the world, but I know, deep down, somewhere hidden inside, that Nathan is losing his way.

I can see it every time my tone gets too blunt, or I snap when he asks me a question, and he has to snake his arms around me and suggest that maybe it's time for another "first date." He watches for my signs, that I'm starting to go dark, and he sees that I get what I need. It's only partly for my benefit, the rest is all self-preservation. Nathan wouldn't survive if I don't get what I need at the right time. It never used to matter if I went a few days without feeding the monster; now, with him, it matters all the more.

I try to push the thought away, but ever since the night he left me, half bound to the kitchen counter, a meat cleaver protruding where the binds had been severed, he has worn this look of acceptance. There is love within it, I know, but when I found him, in a borrowed sweater, sitting on the sidewalk at the end of the street, I knew he had nowhere else to go. What is there to live for when all you've been living for is complete? When his mission to retrieve his mother's cross, the cross that never leaves his neck, was complete, when Danny's killer was confronted, I was all that was left to go to. He didn't choose me, I know. I was just the better option than a road toward nothingness and a life alone. I don't blame him for that. But I know it takes a toll on him.

Which in turn takes a toll on me.

We sleep well into the evening, and he has a bounce of guilty excitement when he remembers the discs he took from last night's kill. And curled up on the sofa, lazy like dogs after a big feed, we watch some graphic horror flick that makes him jump with fear and excitement, makes him yelp with surprise. It's the closest I've seen to genuine happiness since that day on the observation platform, looking down onto the city below in miniature.

Who knew love could be this hard? For me, the highs are worth it.

For him, I'm not so sure.

I'm sitting at my desk in the back office three days later, doodling the image of a caricature hipster being strangled to death with a plastic cord, when my cell rings and the detective addresses me by name. A cold clip of anxiety makes a beeline down my spine. This is new ground, a first to me after all these years, and I start to sweat a little beneath my arms.

His name is Detective Caldicott, he's with the NYPD, and he wants to ask me a few questions about a bar I was drinking in over the weekend.

And it dawns on me, and I realize I'd made a mistake.

For the first time in years, I'd make the one simple slip up that could get me embroiled in something I couldn't talk my way out of; I'd used my credit card at the bar.

Nathan had taken too long trying to pick what to wear and we wanted to get there early enough so I could have a good selection of guys to pick from and when the cab dropped us off a few streets over, Nathan was cold because he didn't bring a jacket. So, we didn't get a chance to hit up the ATM and went straight there.

It's the first time I ever let this happen, but years of complacency and Nathan by my side and I guess I thought I was unstoppable. But every train arrives at its destination eventually.

And Detective Caldicott, he says: "Am I right, Mr. Mallory, in saying you were at the Death-head Moth on Avenue A on the night of May 27th?"

And I take a beat and I reply: "Yes, I went for a few drinks, arrived around ten-thirty." I purposefully exclude mention of Nathan being there, as if the lie can protect him. He's my partner and lives in my house. All it would take is one rudimentary background check to find him.

And I play dumb, like I have no idea what he wants to ask me, and I say: "Can I ask what this is about, Detective?"

His response is clipped and formal, like he's reading from a script, like these bits of information have been recounted several times in quick succession.

And I breathe a silence sigh of relief. I know he has no idea what I did to this guy, when he says: "After attending the bar that night, a gentleman by the name of Jericho Rowland was murdered in his apartment in Queens. We are looking for more information about his whereabouts after he left the bar." The underarms of my work shirt are sodden, stained dark blue with sweat against the baby blue cotton.

The Death-head Moth has no surveillance system, I made sure of that before we went there, it was part of the reason I chose the place. It's a dark as hell punk-type hipster bar, so the lights are so low you could barely make out the face of the guy standing next to you at the bar, soaking the elbows of their band sweater in cheap watered-down vodka or pretentious draft IPA.

And of course, this assholes name was Jericho.

And I ask: "Can you tell me more about this guy? What he looks like?"

I use the present tense, something I read is meant to distance you from the act of murder, which adds an element of denial to your answers like you're not talking about something with the magnitude of ending a man's life. It's a small thing, but it helps.

Caldicott sighs and says: "Six foot one, brown hair to his chin, one of those Groucho Marx mustaches. Wearing a woolen hat and vintage clothing." And he sighs again.

I say: "With all due respect, Detective, you've just described everyone who ever drinks at the Moth."

And he laughs and says: "Yeah, been hearing that a lot."

He has nothing, it's obvious. All I am to him is a name on the credit card receipt from that night, one of maybe one hundred guys who were all there when this Jericho guy was marked for death. They have no murder weapon; I took it with me. They have no suspects, because with no camera footage and the turnover of clientele there at the Moth,

I'm just a name in a list of hundreds who might have seen something they weren't looking out for.

Admittedly, it's jarring. This is the first time one of my marks has ever come with a follow up from law enforcement, and only the second time anyone has followed up at all. The first of course being Nathan, and that changed my life. This? Well, this doesn't look like it'll have the same effect. Hell, if there's any such thing as luck, this will never come up again; it'll just be some ratchet hipster relegated to an obit in the back of the local rag.

Caldicott thanks me for my time and asks me to scrawl down his number, "in case you remember anything," he says, all hope lost in his voice.

And that's all there was.

And when I finish work, I drive by an ATM, and I withdraw three-hundred dollars, the max my card will allow, so I don't have to worry about this ever again.

CHAPTER TWENTY ONE

Next, I killed a guy we picked up at a drinks mixer for endangered whatever at his luxury apartment with the surprisingly lo-fi security systems. Nathan wandered round, inspecting this guy's possessions like he wanted to jam it all in his pockets. When he suggested he wanted to fuck Nathan while I watched, I took his best-in-business trophy, a big, heavy-pointed thing that looked razor-sharp, and jammed it in his meaty neck. Nathan pocketed an antique-looking fountain pen, and I watched as this guy bled a river of hot, wet crimson all over the marble floor of this expensive condo for the aging queer. From what I remember, he was forty-three, and money makes monsters of us all, so it was his time to go. Nathan didn't spare a look at the carnage and made me wipe my feet on the bearskin rug to clean the blood off my dress shoes before we left. Somehow, I managed to smuggle the trophy out, wrapped in the pocket square he was wearing, and tucked impossibly inside my tuxedo jacket.

Then about a week later, I beat some street performer to death with his guitar in an underground parking lot. He'd been playing these awful, faux-British accented covers of Dylan and McCartney and Simon, and the noise had settled in my ears like a swarm of bees. He was singing *Blowing in the Wind* and *In My Life* and *Something So Right*, which usually I would love, but covered in this guy's nasal whine, it drove me crazy. And the monster had stirred. Nathan had seen how I reacted, and made eyes at the guy, luring him to a place where no one else was around, a derelict parking lot under a disused high rise, with only a few cars and no working security cameras overhead. And when I'd pushed this guy to the ground, Nathan opened his guitar case and handed me the guitar, and I'd smashed the guy's head in until there was nothing there but a mass of bloody bone and hair. I beat him so hard that the telecaster body of the electric guitar severed from its neck. Nathan then pocketed all the change from the inside of his guitar case and walked away. As a parting gift, I shoved the splintered neck of the guitar straight through the gaping hole I'd created in his skull. It stood up like a spoon in a jar of thick jelly.

Then there was a vagrant I killed with a sock full of loose coins under a bridge in the early morning hours. That one, I'll admit, was cruel, the change in the sock was all he had to his name, and it was heavy and leaden and managed to knock his teeth out and break his nose into his brain with a few quick swings. The coins in the sock were all we could find to take as a trophy, and Nathan looked away the whole time, unable to watch or see me take the last remnants of this old drifter's life from him in the cruelest of fashions.

And Nathan is there for every one of these, gradually blanching the more abstract, the more gruesome the kills got. And the kills get more gruesome because he's there, and though I know the effect they are having on him, that he isn't cut out for watching the way I operate, I find myself needing more and more to kill in these grotesque and violent ways and I need him to be there to watch.

And the more he watches, the less he can look at me. And it makes me need the kills more, this captive audience of one, chained to watching me portray these living acts of evil on a stage made just for him. He was a theatre kid, forced to watch this macabre Vaudeville show he never asked to see. The price of admission was gradually rising. I could see it in his eyes, on the rare occasion he would meet my gaze.

And then we get home, and it's like he's turned off a part of his mind that associates me with that person, the person who can kill for fun, without remorse, and with increasingly inspiring methods, each time collecting a memento of a fun night or day spent. And the door to our apartment closes, and he's the old Nathan again, the one who loves me.

It's like he's splitting in two, dissociating every time we leave the confines of our shared space, donning a mask that prevents him from taking on board all the sickness that comes with being the love of a killer.

But I know for sure that he sleeps with that curved, solid silver cheese knife, the one he used to gore his only victim to death in the park, slipped under the bed on his side. The knife's not for me, I know. It's just for him, a memento of the one time he had the strength to take a life when it was needed most. It either makes him feel safe, or it lets him know that if the time comes again, he could always lift it and use it when threatened. The fact that it never leaves the under space of our bed, well, I try not to think about that too hard.

And even though he's starting to come apart, and I can't seem to be able to stop myself from edging him there, a part of him still realizes that I pose a danger.

And that one day, he might just have to fight for his life.

I would never hurt him. He knows this somewhere deep inside, but that doesn't stop the fact that sometimes, you must put yourself first.

The cheese knife is the totem that shows him he has an out when he needs it, a safety net when the darkness gets too close.

And when you share a bed with the darkness, it's good to have that contingency in place.

CHAPTER TWENTY TWO

AND JUST LIKE ANYTHING GOOD, it all had to eventually end.

Tonight's date is a young actor, a guy in his early twenties, maybe even Nathan's age, who took a shine to us both as we cruised the darkened dance floor of an underground club. He has this straw blonde shoulder-length hair, and he tells us he auditioned for a few pilots a few months back but has yet to hear if any have been picked up. He says one was a big deal, with some famous actors we might recognize, and reels off a list of names I've never heard before.

His eyes are wide with the force of whatever substance is coursing through his veins, whatever new party drug the kids are taking these days. I ask Nathan: "Molly?" because that's the only one I know from experience. Nathan shakes his head and says: "Nah, GHB," and slurps another vodka soda with lime.

It's a short walk back to the kid's apartment, some fifth-story walk-up with flaking paint on the door frames and rusted fire escapes too unsafe to use should a fire erupt.

He tells us he doesn't live alone but not to worry because his roommate is out of town until Monday. It's like a song to my ears. As soon as he unlocks the door and closes it behind us, he shucks himself out of his tight t-shirt and reveals smooth lean muscle like a swimmer and a tan that wouldn't look out of place in LA. I see, for just a second, Nathan appraises the perfect, golden skin of this gorgeous kid, and the monster inside me stirs.

He forces Nathan up against a wall, gives me a wink and a smile. The actor is promising me a show, that begins with grinding his groin against my lover's, kissing him deeply and passionately. Nathan doesn't close his eyes, as he does with me. I hear him groan in pleasure.

A new rage fills me in that second.

I grit my teeth and watch as this kid dares to unbuckle Nathan's pants with one hand while the other wraps around his throat. Soon Nathan's pants pool around his ankles, and I can tell through the thin fabric of his boxers that he's hard.

Everyone is in danger from me.

This kid frees Nathan's cock from his boxers, and it bounces with the liberation, and as my jaw works in this blind fury, I look Nathan in the eye, and a single tear trickles down the side of his face. He sees the monster approach.

Before the kid can swallow Nathan, I grab a handful of that long blonde hair, and smash the boy's face into the door frame of the shitty shared apartment. I watch his nose explode in a concentric wave of gore.

Nathan tries to move away, but I hold him where he is, then grab the kid's head and smash it again until his glossy lips split. And again, until his teeth crack and dislodge. And again, and again and again, until his face has all but caved in and the hair in my hand has ripped out in clumps. The kid makes no sound as he dies, the shock, horror, and drugs rendering him mute.

But Nathan stands there, right where I made him stand, and tries not to look as this kids blood and bone and cartilage shatters and sprays down the side of his naked leg, landing in thick clumps of gore and chips of calcium in the seat of his boxers and the pants around his ankles.

And Nathan is crying, but I don't care. I repeatedly slam what's left of this dead actor's disintegrating head into this wooden doorframe. I let the corpse collapse to the floor in a wet thud, all mass of beaten flesh making this sickening plop as it hits the hardwood and starts bleeding out of every wound on every part of what used to be his beautiful face.

And when Nathan closes his eyes, I grab him by the hair and force him to look. I say: "You see what happens? What happens when someone touches what is mine?"

And Nathan cries. And he says over and over, "I'm sorry."

I look at what I've done here. This wasn't some compulsion, some demon that lives inside me that needed out. This was all jealousy.

And I don't blame Nathan, and the cruelty of trying to make him apologize for this is overwhelming. My breath steadies and my heartrate slows. He remains crying and whispering a mantra of "I'm sorry."

I pull him close to bury his damp face against my chest, and I say: "Don't worry. I won't let another one abuse you again."

But his tears don't stop, and I must hold him for what feels like hours until his body stops trembling with the fear and sorrow that I caused.

When he's able to pull his pants up over the gore splattered across the hairy skin of his legs, I take him home to where I know he should be able to dissociate who I am from my actions.

Should be.

The night ends early, and we are on the couch at opposite ends, mute and unresponsive. Tonight, was different. Too violent, too personal. Too much of myself and not enough of the darkness to blame. And the darkness wasn't fed tonight. It was just me, and my blinding rage.

We sit on the couch and watch an old movie on mute, with the silence a terrible atmosphere, until I might scream. But the buzzer to my apartment rings, three short mechanical screams. Nathan's body remains as stills as a mannequin though his eyes widen to become small moons.

I go to the intercom and hold one finger to my lips to signify that Nathan needs to keep quiet. When I speak into the box on the wall, I'm staring at my lover. "Hello?"

"Mr. Mallory." And Caldicott's voice is immediately recognizable through the tinny speaker of the intercom. "This is Detective Caldicott with the NYPD. We briefly spoke a few weeks ago."

A single tear drops from Nathan's eye, and he covers his mouth with both hands like he's stifling a scream. I never told him about the previous call, I didn't think it warranted worrying him for no reason, but now in the moment, he sees the deception, what it could mean, and that it's come knocking on our door.

And I say: "Detective, of course, I remember. What can I do for you?"

"Can I come up?"

There's a rustling over the speaker, and I know that Caldicott is not alone.

And I can say nothing more except: "Of course," and I ring the buzzer to release the door.

I walk over to Nathan, and he has stopped breathing entirely and has folded his legs under his chin, his stare boring holes into the fabric of his pants. There's a dark spot on one of the legs where the guy's earlier unwashed remains started seeping through the fabric. He's in no shape to face the police, and just the look of him, with the dark smear down his leg, is enough to put us straight behind bars for the rest of his life.

I keep my voice low and calm, take his arms in my hands. I say to him: "Go into the bedroom. Don't turn the light on. Lie down on the floor. Don't move a muscle until I tell you it's okay to move."

His eyes are wide and vacant, shock setting in. How much of that look is from the current situation, and how much still lingering from how I punished him earlier? Despite the cause, there's a lancet of guilt piercing my gut as I watch him nod that he's understood and push him hard towards the bedroom. I watch as he silently opens the door and closes it again behind him, sparing only a second to meet my eye before he is lost to the other room and the darkness within.

I stare at the wooden panel a second after he disappears and wait for the rap at the front door, a casual, calm knock, like the kind a friend might make when arriving expectedly.

I take a deep breath, cross the floor to the front door, unlock it loudly, and swing it open.

Under the halogen glare of the stairwell's overhead strip lights and surrounded by the acrid smell of fresh smoke and marijuana from the basement student apartment, Detective Caldicott is nothing like I imagined him to be.

He smiles this bright smile, matching the wattage of the overhead light, and reaches out to clasp my hand. He says: "Mr. Mallory," and it's not a question. "Thank you for letting us in at this late hour. I expect this is not how you imagined spending your night."

Though polite, there is something vaguely threatening about his words, all hidden beneath this external veneer of jovial kindness and professional swagger. Despite the heat, he's wearing this long brown trench coat that's seen better days, the buckle swinging at his side broken and functionless, either through lack of care or lack of caring. I view this simply because of the way his gun causes the muddy-brown fabric to tent where it sits at his hip, highlighting the weapon and drawing the eye to it like it's some kind of protective totem. In all fairness, that's exactly what it is.

And I notice that he's younger than I thought he would be, though still a decade my senior, his brown skin taut and smooth, only the crows' feet around his eyes belying the toll of the job. He's Danny Glove in *Lethal Weapon*, the early one's when he was a young guy in the throes of the action, a spry forty-one-year-old providing the responsible foil for a youthful Gibson before he went mad.

And he's wearing these burgundy suspenders over an off-white, near-yellowing shirt, and without permission, my mind unbuckles them, wraps them around his thick neck, and pulls until his eyes bulge wide. It turns out Caldicott is the type of guy I would relish killing before there was Nathan before my routine grew and metastasized into something much darker than I ever thought it could.

Flanking the detective, two uniforms with shoulders like linebackers stand to either side of him and make no move to enter my apartment as Caldicott lets one foot cross the threshold uninvited. And Caldicott says: "Mind if I come in?" as he's halfway inside, the question rhetorical.

Caldicott lets his eyes wonder over every surface, taking in every detail, looking for nothing in particular but cataloguing it all behind those weary eyes for later. I try to see what he's seeing but the familiarity of home makes it impossible.

"Is Mr. McGuire at home?" he asks, leaving the door open to the officers who remain in place.

I think of Nathan lying in the darkness a room over, and I hope that Caldicott doesn't produce a warrant from beneath the brown raincoat. My blood starts to hammer audibly through my veins at the mention of Nathan's name; it sounds like a curse coming from his mouth. He knows who Nathan is, which I still need to account for. I don't know how, but somehow, Caldicott has been digging into us. Nathan has been living here for six months, and though no mail arrives, he often orders food here on Post Mates under his name. And I remember my name on Nathan's discharge documents from the hospital, my signature, my details as his emergency contact. All of this points neon arrows to the guy, and it rocks me slightly that it's not just my ass on the line here.

And I lie to him and say: "He's in the city with friends tonight." My voice doesn't falter, and the lie is stone truth, as I've trained it to be.

"Can I sit?" he asks, hovering by the armchair, and before I can answer, he sits his flabby ass down in my armchair, which only I have ever sat in, and I think, regardless of how this pans out, I'll need a new chair.

I sit in Nathan's spot on the couch and run my hands over the knees of my slacks, wiping away the traces of nervous sweat I didn't know I could produce. He's shaken me, and I don't like it.

And I say to him: "So I take it there has been some news in your case, Detective?" and give a half smile, geniality muted by professional respect and personal curiosity. When I do this, I see my face in my mind, the practice of training my features to deadpan or elicit emotion on command doing me justice when it counts.

His veneer starts to crack as he steeples his fingers and leans his elbows on his knees, drawing his face closer to where I'm sitting. Menacingly but with the utmost confidence, he says: "Why don't you tell me?"

I train my face again, make it look as natural as possible, and respond with an even voice: "I'm not sure I know what you're implying."

Caldicott guffaws and sits back in the seat. Quickly his good ol' boy persona returns, and he says: "Would you be willing to come down to the station and answer some questions?"

I gulp, and I agree because I have no reason to refuse. And because I need to get him away from Nathan.

I HAD OFFERED TO TAKE my car to the station, but Caldicott had insisted on driving me in his cruiser and then tortured me with a resounding silence the whole way there. He didn't force me into the back seat like a suspect; he simply let me sit up front with him while the ever-present officers followed closely behind.

I'm sitting in this tinder block cell with no windows and a low-hanging strip light flickering like a horror movie. I've been alone in here since we arrived, and I can feel insidious eyes watching me from beyond the two-way mirror that spans the length of the east wall. I watch my mannerisms through my periphery without looking directly at the mirror.

Despite everything, despite all the things I've become, I've never been in a police interrogation room before, nor have I been into a police station. The homicide department of the Queens precinct is a low-budget disaster that looks like it's never been awarded a cent of government cash for improvement or incentive. The whole building smells like burnt toast and body odor. The flickering lights start a headache behind my eyes, but I don't lose focus. Too much is riding on my ability to lie out of this, but much like my crimes, I have no plan to do this. The only thing I do have is the ability to adjust at the drop of a hat, and I'm crossing every finger and toe I have that I'm able to spin whatever they have on me on the fly convincingly.

No truths. No lawyers. Just me and whatever comes out of my mouth, which is as dry as a California drought.

After another thousand hours pass, Caldicott enters the room holding a brown paper case file. His sleeves rolled up to the elbow, the shitty Columbo coat no longer draped around him, poorly hiding where his gun is holstered. Now the gun is in full view, gleaming under yellow strip light like a mirror ball, flickering with the broken haunted electrics overhead. Without meeting my eye, his face stripped of benevolence that might have existed when he arrived at my apartment, the detective pulls the seat across the small table from me and slumps into it. The plastic groans under the effort. His armpits have sweat concentrically drying yellowed stains down his shirt, and in the stark faltering light of the room, there is a yellow band around his collar. I wonder when he changed it last, but I don't care.

Caldicott leans forward, his head hovering over the file folder and looks me square in the eye and says: "Last chance. How did you know Jericho Rowland?"

I don't need to lie to answer the question, and I say: "I don't know him."

He sighs and opens his file folder, a glossy print of the late hipster in his living glory, smiling at some yonder wonder in some Insta-filtered photo op.

And it's time to start lying, to draw my inner Keyser Soze out and to deal with this for good. I hesitate over the photograph, asking permission to view the image up close and round the right way. Caldicott nods, and I take the image, spin it on the shining tabletop and wrinkle my brow inquisitively. "This is him?" I ask, and silently the detective nods. And I say: "Looks familiar. But then, so does everyone in the Moth."

I look back at Caldicott, and he moves closer as he tells me to look again.

I study the picture for a fraction longer, how I imagine someone might when staring at the image of a stranger.

Caldicott rolls his eyes and slides a second photo across the table to me. In it, the grainy image taken from CCTV footage shows the guy from the photo getting into a cab, with Nathan and I standing right behind him, moving to join him in the vehicle.

"Does that jog your memory at all?"

I keep my voice calm and try not to react. And I say, "Well, we shared a cab with a guy that night, Detective, but I couldn't tell you anything about him. We'd had a few drinks, and all I remember is dropping off someone and then the cab taking us home."

Caldicott exhales impatiently. "Be that as it may," he says. "It's looking like you and Mr. McGuire are the last two people to have seen the victim alive."

He doesn't have enough to keep me; I know it now. One grainy photo of us with someone looking like this murdered fuckwit is all he's got, and it's all I need to cut this off before it gets too far. So, I say: "Last I checked, Detective, it's not a crime to hail a cab home?"

I know I'm baiting him, and I know I shouldn't, but he's barking up the right tree by accident, and I can't let him have the last laugh. I'm a fucking serial killer. I made some errors in judgment that night, but I'm not the man this detective thinks I am. All he has is a theory rooted in an image of three men getting into a vehicle in the dark.

Caldicott stares daggers at me, his gaze boring deep into the center of my eyes, and I refuse to blink. And after a second of his chewing the inside of his cheek, he leans closer and says: "I think you know more than you're letting on, Mr. Mallory. I think you know what happened to Jericho Rowland. If I find out that you've been keeping that from me, my next visit will include a pair of tight handcuffs. For you…and for Mr. McGuire as well."

The threat causes the hair on the back of my neck to stand on edge, not because I'm worried, but because I believe him. Because the detective has the same relentless drive, I do to get what he wants, I can tell he wants me for this. I know he knows, and I can see it in his eyes; he doesn't believe a word I'm saying. I'm in the spotlight for the first time, not watching from the periphery like some onlooker, unaffected and unseen, but the star of the goddamn show.

And I look at his suspenders, and I know I must do something I shouldn't even consider doing because it would raise a flag over my head and push this investigation further in my direction, and with me, in Nathan's direction. But I have no choice. I'm cornered.

There's not enough to keep me, and I make nice as long as I can before they let me out onto the streets of Queens, the light of very early morning starting to illuminate the sky.

The detective's parting words are: "Don't leave town. And let Mr. McGuire know we'll be in touch."

I think about walking home, but I know I need to get there sooner; I know I need to be with Nathan, now more than ever.

And now, I must kill the detective.

I hail a cab and arrive home as the first shards of sunlight pierce the sky.

CHAPTER TWENTY THREE

THERE IS NOTHING BUT AN eerie silence inside the apartment, but I didn't expect anything else. I don't switch on the lights, hesitate, or train my ear for footsteps because I know precisely where Nathan will be.

And I'm right, of course, when I find him lying on the bedroom floor in the dark, right where I told him to stay. And I realize the way he loves me, that he would do anything I ask of him. And I recognize the way I love him and would move heaven and hell for him to keep him out of the grips of someone like Caldicott.

Nathan is sleeping when I crouch beside him, his gentle breaths coming out in ragged pants, his eyes darting behind his closed lids in REM sleep. It's a shame to wake him, but I do, gently shaking him out of slumber until he awakes with a start, a panic-stricken look invading the sweet innocence of his face. His eyes adjust to the semi-dark, and he finds my face, relaxes, pulls me down on top of him, and kisses me deeply, both of our mouths dry and sour, our breath the mingling scent of decay.

And he tells me: "I had a dream they took you away, and you were never coming home." And he starts to cry.

I fall back onto my knees, reach my hands beneath his sobbing body and haul him up from the floor, up into my arms, and carry him out into the lounge where I sit him in his spot on the couch, the one still imprinted with the dent of my ass where I was forced to sit there earlier. When I sit, I sit next to him and not in my chair. I won't sit in that chair again.

There's a frosty atmosphere coating the apartment like our private bubble made for us had burst. Nathan is shaking like he's about to freeze to death, and I try to comfort and pull him into my arms, but he pushes me away. And he unfurls himself, and in a wave of anger and fear, he yells: "The police had spoken to you before?" And I put on my taking charge voice but still maintain my loving affection for him. I tell him: "Calm down. They just wanted to know if I knew anything about the guy who was killed. They've got nothing except we were there and shared a cab. That's all."

I reach for him in vain, as his hands push mine away.

And he says, "And what happens when they track that cab journey that never went beyond his place?"

And I can't respond because I don't have an answer. I didn't need one sitting face-to-face with Caldicott, and I won't need one again if I can just deal with him how I need to.

My mouth makes shapes, but no words come out. I'm like a fish out of water, gasping and grasping for a lifeline I can't quite reach. And I close my mouth and don't say a thing.

He crumples and puts his head in his hands.

And I try to console him, but my tone is all off, from the night's events, from the talk with the police, and because, most of all, I'm afraid; afraid this is it, that I've gone as far as I can go without consequences; worried that I only got six months with Nathan before losing everything.

And I understand how Nathan felt the night he came here to kill me.

He picks up my cell and puts it in his pocket, and I don't try and stop him. I know he'll want to be the one to see if the detective calls again. I've lost his trust for not telling him about the first call.

And then he walks away into the bedroom and slams the door. I hear its little rickety lock close, and beyond that, I listen to him sweep everything from the dresser in anger.

I fight the urge to follow him because I know it'll do no good.

And I try to figure out how to get us out of this, praying to any god that will listen for a way to save us both.

First, I need a plan, one to find Caldicott and stop his investigation once and for all. Or there's the lesser of the two evils, something I'm not known to do but would do for him: I could pack up everything we have, and we could run.

NATHAN MCGUIRE:

HELL IS EMPTY
AND ALL THE DEVILS
ARE HERE
WILLIAM SHAKESPEARE

CHAPTER TWENTY FOUR

FOR A WHILE I WAS strong enough to keep the darkness at bay, in both of us. But what he needed, eventually became obvious. He was a pressure cooker, and the build-up would have been brutal if I hadn't let him point it elsewhere.

But after the night in the park, the night I saw him beaten and bloodied and overcome on the dirt, I told him he couldn't go out there alone. Maybe that was the biggest mistake I made in the long laundry list of epic mistakes. He tailored his kills to suit me, and used me as a lure to pull them in. I was complicit.

I didn't know how often he would need to let off the pressure, but I couldn't say anything about it, because it stopped being about the thrill for him, and instead it became about keeping me shielded from his violence. It was love, as fucked up as it was. I knew that. He knew that.

But it turns out, his darkness was a cancer, one that poisoned me. There was so much of it, that even the light of our time alone together, in our apartment, where we could be just us, like any other normal couple, wasn't enough to make it worth it.

It was all temporary.

And I knew he would kill me if I left. And I knew if I left it would kill me.

So, I stayed.

The kills got worse. They got so bad I couldn't close my eyes without seeing the blood and the gore. I had to stop watching him most of the time, because instead of his loving smile, all I saw was these red hands dripping in the gore of unsuspecting victims.

But the worse it got, the less I was able to function. He had to remind me to wash and change my clothes. He had to keep an eye on me so that he knew I was eating.

What started off feeling like a home, quickly turned into a prison.

So, I gave up. It wasn't a life.

Then, tonight, when the blonde-haired actor kissed me, I saw a window into the real Jake, and what looked back at me was not the kind of love I had stayed around for. It was wild and jealous, not the face of his monster, but Jake's face, a monster all along. And the way he had made me look at the wreckage of his victim, as if I had somehow asked for any of this, as if I was somehow to blame, that was a new look on him. It wasn't a good look.

Now I can't even stand to look at him because I've seen too much. I looked death in the face and survived, but when that same force is wearing the face of the one you love, it's time to just close your eyes and never open them again.

Love does crazy things to you.

I could have sat on that couch forever, basked in the finite moments of light when he would look at me and I would feel what it must have been like to be cherished. It was unlike any drug I'd ever taken.

Then the detective arrived and took him away, and the whole thing came crashing down. It was the final straw, the one that broke the camel's back. Police don't just drop by for casual visits or take you downtown to question you for fun. We were tied to Jericho Rowland now, and it was only a matter of time before they fit the rest of the pieces together. There will be a warrant to search the apartment and they'll find every shred of evidence they need secreted away beneath the loose floorboard in the closet.

Hell, there's even a dried patch of evidence sticking my jeans to my leg right now. I fight the bile rising in my throat and decide it's over. I decide, in that moment, that I'm done.

So, I get up, I take his cellphone, and I walk into the bedroom and lock the door behind me.

It's the beginning of the end, and it can't come soon enough, for both of us. It was always going to end; I just didn't see it ending like this.

CHAPTER TWENTY FIVE

I KEEP THE KNIFE I'D used to kill that man in the park tucked safely beneath the bed, within reach should I ever need it, and when I pull it out, it feels like it belongs in the palm of my hand. It is heavy and soothing, a weight that feels at home though my hand still shakes in what can only be described as shock. And I chastise myself for letting shock take me over. How did I think this would really go?

The knife gleams under the table lamp light, and I have cleaned it so thoroughly that no remaining traces of blood still cling to its monstrous teeth, but when I blink, I can still see it there, the terrible gore of my one and only kill dripping down my wrists and onto the floor. And I can't unsee it.

Out damned spot.

The summer night is silent as I retrieve Jake's cell from my pocket, scan the contacts list and find the number listed for Detective Caldicott.

When I send the call, it takes me directly to the precinct front desk, and I say: "I'd like to confess to a murder."

I tell them everything, the guy in the park, the hipster, Jericho Rowland, some musician, a busker, a vagrant, the actor who we killed tonight, and every other terrified face I can still see looping through my brain on repeat; I give all the details to the clerk on the phone. I share their names because even though I know, Jake doesn't remember a single one of them, not really, I remember them all. I remember their faces and the fear in their eyes as they died. Even though I had to look away, I saw enough to commit the act to memory and heard enough never to stop being able to hear a death cry up close. I cannot forget a detail, no matter how hard I try. I am not gifted in the same way I was when I was a kid being abused by the people my brother invited into our lives, and I can't hide those memories in some lockbox inside my head.

I didn't wield the murder weapon, but my silence and acceptance were all I needed. I was complicit, and I helped to kill these men, and there is no doubt about that. The last six months of kills are all my body count.

The desk clerk tells me he will transfer me to Caldicott, and I tell him not to bother. I tell him the address, and then I hang up.

I listen for Jake but hear only silence.

When I'm sure he's not about to bust the lock and come in after me, I take up the knife and finish the job.

JACOB MALLORY:

HELL, OR HIGHWATER

THE BURLINGTON WEEKLY
HAWK EYE
MAY 1882

CHAPTER TWENTY SIX

I'M TRYING FOR PATIENCE AS I wait for him to come back. I convinced myself it would be fine, and we got out at this guy's place to walk home and see the sunrise. There's nothing to tie us to his apartment, and I'd bet my left leg he won't be able to make it stick. But then I see the determination in Caldicott's face, the way he swore he would come after us, and my heart drops.

I walk to the kitchen, pull the vodka out of the cupboard, pour a shot, and drink it to burn my throat.

I'm pouring another when I hear the bedroom door unlock and hear his slow, somehow defeated footsteps on the hardwood. I take the shot and prepare to fight to keep my life; he is all it has amounted to. And it's like he always says: "It's not nothing."

As he emerges from the hallway, the motion sensor picks up his slowed movements, and the light overhead engages.

Nathan is holding the damn silver cheese knife in one hand, though barely.

And his skin is open from wrist to elbow, deep in the left wrist, less so in the right, the blood pouring like thick syrup down his pale skin, down the silver tinge of the ornate knife, and onto the floor in gore and gushes.

And I stand there.

I've seen blood before, but not his, not like this. The sight is too much, and I can't bare it. This must be how it feels for him to watch me kill. And I feel my heart break. For him, for me.

I grab a blanket from the couch. I try to wrap Nathan's arms and swaddle the gashes, but too much blood has reached the floor from the new cracks in his flesh.

And I start to cry. I haven't wept in years, but I'll never stop.

His face is pale, and his eyes are distant, and I'm screaming: "What did you do? Nathan, what have you done?"

And I look around for my cell phone, and it's not there because he's taken it, and I'm crying, real tears I had no idea I was capable of, wet animalistic sobs just pouring out of me like thunderclaps in the silence of our home.

And with a broken voice, Nathan whispers: "I called the police. They're on their way."

The blood soaks the fabric between us. It won't stop. And he says: "You can't save us both."

He collapses to the floor, too empty, too far gone to stand anymore, and I pull him close, hold him, and weep for everything he gave me that was all going away.

The silver knife clatters to the floor, and in that second, I know it's over, that it all caught up to me. And I think back to when I first met Nathan, that day in the hospital where he lured me to his bedside. I think of how I vowed to build him back up and destroy him for my amusement.

And how well I succeeded, but I'm not amused. I'm devastated.

He says: "There's still time to run. You could start over somewhere else."

And I cry: "I'm not leaving you."

And he says: "You can still get away." And I can't form words. I cry, shake my head, and hold him close as if my embrace could hold in whatever blood remains in his veins.

His head lulls, and he whispers: "I really did love you."

The blood is running thinner now. There's not enough left inside Nathan. It's all pooled around him, and there's so much. And he closes his eyes, and he is gone.

And I scream this raw scream that tears at my vocal cords, ravages my throat, such painful lost cries I have never heard a man make before. Because, for the first time in my life, I know what it feels like to be the one left behind, the way I made everyone around all my victims feel. I know now how it feels, and I can't stand it.

It takes me a minute to compose myself, to stop the tears and the screams. All the while, I cradle Nathan's dead body in my arms. I don't want to let him go, but he is gone, and I can't bring him back. The best I can do for him now is make it right for anyone who might remember him when he's gone.

I take a pillow from the couch and lay his head on the floor, keeping him comfortable though he is beyond comfort now. Perhaps he always was.

And I lay beside him, curling myself around him, surrounded by all the blood that once pumped through his veins that now sits wasted on the floor of our home.

Eventually, when I'm sodden with his blood, I have a choice. Killing Caldicott would do nothing now. Nathan's cold dead body has ended that plan indefinitely. His call to the police... everything points at my head like a loaded gun.

I could have run like he wanted me to. I wonder if that's why he did this; to give me the option to leave but to save himself from me simultaneously. I could have left him there, got in my car with the $300 cash I keep, and seen how far I could make it before this caught up. But it's not a choice now Nathan's gone.

As I lie there, chilled by the cooling blood seeping through my clothes, I know there is no way I could ever leave him like that.

I get up, walk to the bedroom, retrieve my cell phone, and dial Detective Caldicott's number. He picks up on the first ring.

His agitated voice says: "Mallory, can you hear me?"

And I reply, barely above a whisper, through the pain in my throat: "I killed them all. Nathan had nothing to do with it. It was all me."

And it strikes me just how much death I'm owning up to. It's been years of me picking off these men around the city, all killed in different ways, all with different means so that they never made a pattern."

Unsaid, they were just the casualties of living in a city where the darkness invited monsters. I think of all the trophies in the space beneath the floorboards, and I tell him where he will find them. I doubt he will be able to match them all. There was never an intention to flick back through a filing system. But there's enough to start.

And I hang up the phone and walk back to where I left Nathan, his thick red blood painting angelic wings on either side of his cooling-blued body.

And this is how it was always meant to end; a fitting retribution for everyone I snuffed from this world who might have had a chance to thrive. And that this is the way I was always meant to go, rejoining a human race I had always been shy of, sharing with them in the loss of love that has the power to ruin and destroy.

And now I am destroyed. And I cry again and sit with Nathan, the Shiva to my fallen love, unwashed and unsullied by the outside world. Nothing exists beyond this moment. Not anymore.

And I tell him: "I really love you too," and I sweep my hand across his eyes to close them and tenderly kiss his blued lips, forcing my tongue inside him one final time.

In the distance, sirens break the silence, and I pick up the cheese knife for one last kill. And I drag it across my throat as deep as it will go until it slides with an audible ripple against bone, and feel the wet, warm torrent of my blood cascade down my body, to mix and mingle with Nathan's spilled blood.

I lie down with him and let all my blood go, a last gift to him. With every bit of will that still exists inside me, I will see him on the other side. And as I bleed my blood into him and everything goes black, I think we see our monsters meet, and together they dance in the dark. A vampire, sucking the life from those around him, sways against the boy made of a thousand broken pieces, all stitched together and animated by electricity. I want this romance to last, but it all ends too soon.

www.ingramcontent.com/pod-product-compliance
Lightning Source LLC
Chambersburg PA
CBHW032020050726
47590CB00006B/2245